A STIRRING IN THE BONES

A STIRRING IN THE BONES

JENNIFER LYN PARSONS

LUNA STATION PRESS

NEW JERSEY

 LUNA STATION PRESS

576 Valley Road #197
Wayne, NJ 07470
lunastationpress.com
info@lunastationpress.com

For Braveheart, Chess, and Underfoot

without them, Learza would have no voice

A STIRRING IN THE BONES

Prologue
The stirring begins

Sunlight rarely found its way to the lowest, shambling levels of Torant City. In winter, even those few shafts that made the long journey failed to drive away the chill. With evening descending, one of those elusive beams of light filtered through the dank to illuminate an old woman dressed in a simple housecoat, worn slippers on her feet. Shivering in the icy, still air, she laid out cracked bowls of food from the pile in her arms. Alley felines, mewling as they circled her legs, rubbed against her as she spoke to them in chatty, admonishing tones.

"Now Nutty, ya leave Tato alone an' let her eat." she paused, listening for a moment. "I dinna care who stole who's food last night. Ya just eat yer own now."

She sighed into the air, "Silly pittins. Ya need ta just get along."

Her daily task complete, she stood and stretched, looking up at the sky. Despite her advanced age, her posture was straight and her movements smooth. "Ring 'round the sun. There'll be snow tonight, no doubt. Glad I got me old furnace fixed. S'ppose it were worth the money then."

With a warm smile on her face, she watched the felines for another moment, listening to their contented crunches and slurps. She was about to leave when a gray tabby stopped eating and jumped over its orange companion, the movement catching the woman's eye. A breath later, another of the colony stopped eating, looked up and moved to the dish abandoned by its brethren.

"Hmm. So, there's change about. Somethin' is shifting." She continued to watch the cats for any further activity. "Now why canna see anythin' else? Tha's odd. Time ta consult another source, I'd say."

Turning away from her charges, she opened the rusty door. Its hinges creaked in protest, catching the cats' attention and a few attempted to follow her inside.

"No, wee ones, not tonight. I've got things ta do." She nudged them out of the way, her hand brushing their silky fur as she pushed them back. "Tomorrow mornin', sweet things, I'll let ya in. Dinna worry."

Once inside she walked the few steps it took to reach the living room, its overstuffed furniture cloaked in shadows. She turned on one dim lamp, then sat on the couch, the worn cushion sinking under her weight. After briefly stretching her shoulders, she reached down to the front of the cabinet that served as a coffee table and opened one of its many drawers.

Various objects sat in neat rows and piles, cushioned by the tray's blue felt lining. The woman slid her hands over the carved objects and decks of cards with a practiced ease. Making her choice, she pulled out a cloth pouch, its purple fabric faded and worn.

The woman lit a few of the candles sitting ready upon the cabinet top, then doused the lamp. Taking the bag into her hands, she moved the contents about inside the rough fabric.

"Yes, yes, there's a shiftin'," she spoke to the air, a soft mumble in the silence of the room.

She began to shake the bag with short, sharp snaps of her wrist. "Alrigh' then, let's see what there is to see, eh?"

She dumped the contents onto the table with a clatter, the irregular shapes bouncing off the old wood, shattering the quiet of the room. Her eyes darted around, taking in the position of each object and its distance from the others.

"Well, well. Hail tha bones," she said, her voice clear and strong now. "I nearly forgot and wouldn't that be a sorry thing? She'll be coming ta the fore soon, tha's right."

As the elusive patterns in the placement of the objects revealed themselves to her, the woman grew more excited. "Ooh, and I'll be havin' visitors, yes tha's right. How could I 've forgotten? Gettin' weak in the brain, me."

"And will ya look at tha'!" Pointing at the smallest of the bones, a satisfied grin spread across her face. "Well, she'll be an interestin' one ta meet, I'll say."

The woman continued to nod and comment on the pale bones before her, their edges smoothed by years of use. "Ah and the Dark One, aye. That'll be the snag there. Oh, and tasks for Grannie Hella as well. Interestin'."

Pausing, she looked up, eyes focused on the blank space in front of her for a long moment before shrugging her shoulders. "Well, I weren't ready for all that movin' about, but things happen as must be and there's naught for me ta do but follow along now, is there?"

One last look around the table and she nodded her head firmly, confirming that she had seen all she needed to see for the time being.

"Well, it'll be a busy time then fer this old body. Best get some rest an' see what I can do ta get m'self ready."

She placed each bone back into the bag and then, moistening her fingers, snuffed out each candle. After a final peek at the felines outside her door, the woman made her way up the creaking, wooden stairs to her bedroom.

Outside the last rays of sunlight had faded to darkness, giving way to grey clouds, pregnant with moisture. The storm rolled in high overhead and wind began to whistle through the vast canyons of steel and stone. The alley cats abandoned their remaining food to scurry for cover as the first flakes made their way to even these forgotten levels of the city. By morning, every surface would be blanketed in icy white snow. Winter in Torant City had begun.

Chapter 1
Disturber of the peace

Stone Sanctuary, Heronat, Morlan Sector

Tir's Blessing connected him to the Two that were One, the All That Is and the All That Was and Shall Be, the Universe and the Void. The balanced energies of the two surrounded him, penetrated him and gave his life meaning. Those within his order said he was near to mastering his connection to this elusive power. The elders told him he was special, that Tir's Great Will flowed through him like a raging river. He knew little of what they meant for he simply heard the voices whisper to him, their soft chorus a beacon in times of indecision and doubt. He followed this song above all others.

For many years now he found his center here in the library. Soft wind carried the sweet smells of the plains through the open windows. It rustled the pages of books left open on low wooden tables by careless initiates. It made him smile and think of his own youth and the connection he shared with these children, the Will of Tir gifting them as equally as it ostracized them from the rest of humanity.

As he moved about the room, retrieving volumes and re-stacking papers, he smiled. War had not reigned across the galaxy in his lifetime, all was at peace. When his task was completed, the fraer placed a cushion in front of the window and folded himself upon it in prayer.

Closing his eyes, he released his fears and his anxieties to the welcoming Void and watched in renewed awe as his inner eye filled with precognitive visions. He observed the patterns of possibility as they shifted and changed, to him like waves breaking upon a beach, rhythmic yet always unique. As he moved deeper into his trance, chanting quietly under his breath, he became aware of a new thread of distortion. A dark path among the peaceful light. It was then that he heard the door creak open and the heavy tread of boots across the stone floor. The sound was accompanied by a stinging, acrid odor.

The fraer did not move, keeping his eyes closed as the intruder approached. Tir sent him no warning signs and all visions of the future went blank before his inner eye. Casting a mental net across the room, the fraer searched for any sign of Tir's Will touching this intruder and felt nothing. The person that interrupted his meditation had not received a Blessing.

"Do you know what I'm here for?" a woman's voice broke the silence, her tone muffled.

When she received no response she came up behind the fraer and nudged him in the back with a cold cylinder of metal. "Come out of that trance and deal with me, monk."

'She comes making demands and desecrates the temple with her technology?' the thought entered his mind and he pushed it aside with ease. Indigence and anger were not the Will of Tir. When his mind was calm and he was at peace once again he opened his eyes.

The fraer rose and faced the intruder. She was tall, wiry and dressed in dark grey, her face hidden behind a mask of ventilators and dark goggles. As the fraer turned, she took a step back, horror betrayed in her body language.

"Are you injured or impaired that you wear that over your face?" he asked her, the sympathy in his voice sincere. "I, too, have injuries that make me unattractive to most people. They say there are treatments that could have cured it, but it is not the way of my order to use such technology."

He put up a hand toward her, the gesture soothing. "It is the Will of Tir that I appear thus, no more, and so I accept it as such."

His awkward smile, appearing half as a frozen grimace, distracted the woman for a moment. With time slipping away, she recovered herself and aimed the blaster at the fraer's chest. "I'm here for the journal of Aedan Kapradina. I know it is here, so no tricks."

The fraer shook his head, concern in his eyes. "I'm sorry, but I cannot let you have that. It will bring no good to our worlds, only darkness."

"Darkness? No, not darkness. Only justice and a balance of power. It will make us all equal." He watched as she shifted her weight back and forth between her feet. The fraer closed his eyes for a brief moment, long enough to sense the life force of the sentinels at the gates ebb to nothing, along the the pain from their wounds. "No longer will you monks be the only ones with access to the power of Tir's Blessing."

"Access? Power?" he questioned her. Her disquiet

betrayed her intent. There was violence in her. He hoped to keep her occupied until help arrived. "All people have Tir's gift of Blessing within them." He shook his head. "You must simply open your heart and listen."

"You believe that if you want, monk." She spit the words at him as if they were poison. "But that mark on your forehead says otherwise." She took a step closer to the ascetic, taking the safety off her blaster. "Now. Give me the journal and you won't have to die."

The fraer paused, his instinctual sense of self preservation taking hold. Long years of practice and faith allowed him to move past this feeling as he released his fears to the Void. "I'm am sorry. It shall not be yours," he told her in a voice untainted by any hint of fear.

"So be it." Her voice held no emotion as she pulled the trigger.

A flash of light blinded him just before the searing heat ripped through his ribcage. A small spot of red began to spread across his blue robes as he fell to the floor. His hands moved down protectively into the folds of fabric, though he made no attempt to staunch the flow of blood. He did not speak as the life drained from his body, but closed his eyes and released the pain with an inner prayer. There was a look of peace upon his face a few moments later when the woman knelt beside him.

"You stupid people never take the easy way out, do you?" she asked the body as she lay her blaster on the floor.

She moved the monk's hands aside and reached into his robes, feeling around inside them for a moment. Her hand stopped as it passed over a rectangular object within.

"Ah, there we are," she grinned beneath the mask. "Your hands moved right to it, did you know that?" she asked the still form as she rifled through the layers of cloth for the hidden pocket.

She pulled out an old book, its once intense, blue cover worn and faded. Standing and stepping away from the fraer's body, she unwrapped the leather strap that secured the covers shut and flipped through a few pages.

"Yes, this is it." She whispered aloud, awe in her voice. "Just a few more things and we'll be ready."

After tucking the book inside her bag, the masked woman grabbed her weapon and hurried toward the door. Sounds of shouting in the distance stopped her in her tracks.

"Damn. Too slow thanks to you," she cursed the man laying prone at her feet.

Running to the open window, she took a deep breath and climbed onto the ledge. The gentle breeze tried to gain entry to her senses, to tease her with the scent of living, growing things, but it could not penetrate her mask. As she shuffled along the precarious outcropping, the woman ignored the zephyr, her concentration focused on the cold metal of the blaster in her hand.

When she reached the ground a short time later, she began running across the plain, careful to stay hidden among the bluffs and gullies that crisscrossed the grassy surface. On her journey she passed a few of the crumbling statues so pervasive in the area, stone monuments to the guardians who abandoned the planet, moving back to Acking long ago.

It took her some time to reach the deteriorating remains

of a settlement rising from the steppes, its crumbling walls casting deep shadows on the spacious courtyard within. A sleek ship, sitting nestled within the enclosed space, fired up its engines as she approached. The door opened and she climbed aboard, ripping off the mask.

"I've got it! Let's go!"

Chapter 2
Along the road

Trans-planetary Space, Morlan Sector, approaching Heronat

Colored lines of light passed by the viewport. A quiet rumble from the interstellar engines soothed the passengers as they slept peacefully in their comfortable quarters. In one of the smallest cabins, a fraer of the Hantirri and his student sat comfortably side by side. The fraer had his legs folded and eyes closed, chanting softly, while the scolyt was entranced by the lights outside their porthole.

'*Sa?*'

The gentle brush on Fraer Elys Ki Dul's mind pulled on his attention. His charge was a good student, but her timing could be a bit off. He had been deep in prayer and now must stir himself out of his trance to answer her probing.

Letting a hint of his frustration show through, he replied. '*Yes, Scol?*'

'*Are we there yet?*' she asked, excited and not seeming to notice the irritated tone of his reply.

'*Almost, young one. Patience, remember?*' he admonished her and gave her a pat, a physical acknowledgment to reinforce his thought-message.

'Yes, Sa.' came the apologetic reply as his companion returned her attention to the viewport.

'Why don't you try to sleep a little?' he offered the thought through the bond they shared.

'The engines are loud, Sa.' she replied.

'Yes, I know you have trouble blocking them out, but you must work on that, Learza.' The thought was sent to her with a wave of encouragement.

'Yes, Sa. I'll try.' she told him, closing her eyes and settling herself more comfortably in her seat.

'No, young one.' he sent her another gentle admonishment. *'Remember, a fraer commits themselves completely to their task, no matter how mundane.'*

She looked up and upon seeing the encouragement in his eyes, returned to her meditation.

A few hours later, the duo arrived on the surface of the planet Heronat and disembarked along with the other passengers. As folk gathered their luggage from the belt that circled around near their gate, the two ascetics strolled in the direction of the exit. They had no bags of their own to retrieve, for their stay would be extraordinarily brief despite all the distance they traveled to get here.

After passing through the gate's entrance, they followed the few scattered passengers from other ships all funneling toward the customs inspection stations. Keeping to the edges of the group, they were able to enjoy the views of the vast grasslands outside the windows that ran from floor to ceiling along the corridor.

'Sa, do you think we'll get to take a walk out there while we're here?' The young scolyt asked, nudging her companion

with a wave of her infectious high spirits.

'If there is time, Scol, if there is time. Remember we are on a mission.' the man replied with his own nudge of calming influence.

The young student was always excited to visit a new spaceport, the sights and sounds and, most importantly, smells drew her attention in a thousand different directions. She had been reminded many times that proper Hantirri behavior did not involve the level of exploration her natural instinct insisted upon. She struggled with this, but usually succeeded in walking side by side with her mentor, eyes focused ahead of her and head held high.

There were not many travelers making their way out to the sparsely populated planet and the line to the customs desk moved quickly. Within a few minutes, Fraer Ki Dul found himself stepping up to the counter and handing over his paperwork to the tight-faced woman across the desk.

She spoke in a bored drone, the tone of one who's repeated the required phrases one too many times for her sanity's well being. "Welcome to Heronat. Paperwork, please."

After a moment she looked up, realizing the documents were already in front of her and met the gentle grin of the Hantirri with a quiet "Hrmph."

'She's unhappy, Sa. She doesn't like her job.' Learza mentally prodded the man standing next to her.

'Be that as it may, Learza, she is doing it properly. Now please be still until we are done here.' The fraer gave his companion a tiny mental nudge that pulled her back into focus.

The woman briefly looked over their traveling credentials, then peeked over the edge of the counter at Learza.

"She'll have to go into quarantine while you're here. It's regulations."

"I'm sorry," the fraer told her. "That's just not possible. She's my student and must be at my side."

"Your student? Well, that's a new one." The woman chuckled under her breath. "Well, I'm sorry too, Mister... uh. Ki Dul" she replied, checking the paperwork for his name.

"Fraer," he informed her.

"What was that?" she questioned in a sharp tone, the correction jarring her out of her mindless routine.

"My apologies. It's Fraer, Fraer Elys Ki Dul. I am Hantirri and she is an initiate of my order." He pointed to Learza who did her best to look friendly.

"Hantirri, huh? Well, be that as it may, it doesn't change the rules," The woman was firm. "She is a dog, Fraer Ki Dul. And dogs from off planet must be quarantined for thirty days or the length of their owner's stay, whichever comes first."

"Please, if you would look over Learza's paperwork again." Elys had grown used to this conversation not long after taking Learza on as his personal scolyt. "I know there is a special dispensation in there from the DHA. It allows Scol Learza to travel freely and bypass the standard quarantines." He emphasized his companion's title, as much for Learza's benefit as the customs officer's.

After their first difficult encounter with officials on Pendar, the Grand Synod made arrangements through the Diot Health Authority for extra vaccinations and regular checkups by a certified veterinarian, allowing Learza to accompany her mentor on missions with less bureaucratic difficulty. Sometimes, in their hurry to process long lines of impatient travelers or simply through their rote complacency, the extra notifications would be overlooked.

"Oh, yes. My apologies, it is here." The woman looked a bit sheepish that she had missed the bright blue sheet of paper, firmly attached to the inside cover of the passport. "Learza, female, aged five, breed unknown. And here, yes, all her vaccinations are in order."

"No apologies necessary, all is sorted now." Elys reassured her. "Are we free to go then?"

"Yes, of course," the official replied, her voice rising into a saccharine tone as she address the young scolyt. "And you'll be a good doggie while you're here won't you, girl?"

The woman sat back in her seat, shock on her face as Learza literally rolled her eyes at the woman and turned away, following her mentor toward the open doorway.

'That woman does not appreciate the Hantirri, Sa. And she thought I was cute.' The mental voice was pouting in tone and tinged with self doubt. *'I'm more than cute, aren't I, Sa?'*

Just outside the spaceport's doors, Elys pulled Learza to the side and knelt next to her.

"It matters not what that woman thinks about you, young one. You are a faithful scolyt of the Hantirri order. Do not forget that." He rubbed the fur around her ears, the action always calmed her. "Remember, most folk this close to the Shambles have never even seen one of our order." He felt her relax and continued to scratch her head. "Do not doubt yourself. Look upon the crystal that you wear about your neck and know that you are Hantirri in truth." His tone carried a weight and confidence with it that Learza would not dare question.

To emphasize his point, Elys gave Learza's garment a little tug. The specially made vest was equipped with a few pockets containing snacks, their papers and their mission documents. A bright blue crystal hanging from the loose chain collar around her neck jingled with the movement.

The physical reminder of her place at her mentor's side brightened Learza's mood instantly. With a quick bark that Elys had come to recognize as her laugh, Learza gave his face a big lick and bumped his shoulder with her head.

"Alright, young one." Elys laughed out loud. "Now that things are settled, shall we take care of this task?"

With another bark, Learza raced a few paces ahead of her mentor as he hastily stood and followed his energetic student.

Chapter 3
Unfriendly waters

Zorziz Spaceport, Heronat, Morlan Sector

The soft winds blowing across the plains brought the clean scent of grasses with them. The smells tickled at Learza's nose, taunting her with the possibilities of new adventures. She was a few steps ahead of Elys when she stopped short, sat on her haunches and inhaled the scents with every cell in her being. Satisfied for the moment that the adventures were there for the taking, she stood back up and returned to her mentor's side.

"Almost lost you to the winds, didn't I, Scol?" he asked her when she stopped, panting, in front of him.

He did not wait for her response, for they both knew the truth of the matter. Learza would always be pulled between the wild world of her instincts and the disciplined world of the Hantirri. It had become enough for them that she made the effort to keep the balance.

Sitting outside the spaceport terminal was a row of five grounders, each with a driver leaning against the door holding a sign. Elys glanced over each vehicle down the line until a young man at the far end caught his attention. He seemed to be actively looking for his fare where his companions were nonchalantly waiting for their customers to locate them instead.

Elys walked toward the driver, Learza at his heel. The young man had a sign reading "Ki Dul", scribbled in black across a sheet of paper. His eyes were focused on the terminal doors and he jumped when Elys approached him.

"Oh! Sir, pardon me!" the young man's voice broke as he stumbled over his words. "Are you the Hantirri? I mean... sorry. Are you Fraer Ki Dul?"

"Yes, I am he. And this is Scolyt Learza," Elys replied, his tone calm and reassuring.

"Oh!" the young driver looked down at Learza, a grin breaking out on his face. "Well, I'm pleased to meet you both. I'm Daki Vanleer. They hired me to drive you to the capitol building."

'Sa, I like him. He is Blessed,' a whisper brushed against Elys's mind.

'Is he really?' Elys scanned the young man quickly, there was a very faint mark at the base of Daki's throat. 'Yes, he is, which would explain his excitement in meeting us.'

'Yes, Sa. Maybe you could train him, too,' the mental nudge was teasing as Learza put her head up under Elys's hand.

The Hantirri looked down at his student and quirked an eyebrow at her. 'I think one scolyt is quite enough, don't you?'

The canine gave no mental response, but nuzzled her head into his hand until he relented and gave her a scratch behind her ears.

"Learza would like you know that she likes you," he told the driver. "You are Blessed, yet your parents did not send you to the Hantirri?"

"No, sir," Daki looked down at his feet as he spoke, his face falling into a frown, "They... well, they don't trust the Hantirri, sir."

Elys sighed, the tale was a familiar one. "I see."

Looking back up, Daki's eyes grew wide and he spoke once more with the enthusiasm of his youth. "I trust you, though. I know the Hantirri are doing everything they can to help rebuild. That's why you're here aren't you?"

"I'm not sure I understand you," Elys replied, confused.

"Well, why else would a Hantirri be all the way out here if it wasn't some important mission? Are you trying to get a new enclave set up here?" The driver bounced a little on the balls of his feet as he spoke. It was reassuring to Elys that there were some folk still willing to openly embrace the Hantirri Order.

"I am sorry to disappoint you, Daki, but I am simply a messenger here to deliver some private papers to your prime minister. No more."

The fraer spoke with a gentle tone and a soft smile on his face, but he noted that Daki's shoulders drooped back down and he stopped bouncing.

"Oh sure, I get it. I just kinda thought I would get to see a different tradition."

"A different tradition?" Elys asked as Learza sniffed around the curb.

Reaching Daki's feet, she stopped her explorations and caught Elys's attention. *'Sa! He knows other Blessed!'*

"Yes, sir," Daki explained to Elys. "The Tirtet have invited me to go on retreat with them next month." Daki's mood brightened once more. "I just hope I'm up for that kind of lifestyle."

'Who is he talking about, Sa?' Learza's prodding was ceaseless once her curiosity was piqued.

"The Tirtet? I was unaware they had an enclave here," Elys replied to Daki before turning his attention to his scolyt.

'They are related to the Hantirri, Learza. They are also Blessed, but they do not use any technology unless its absolutely necessary, nor do they wield weapons. They simply experience the Will of Tir and attempt to attain inner peace,' he explained.

'Maybe they could help you, Sa,' the canine's thought was gentle and encouraging.

Elys looked down into her deep brown eyes. *'Perhaps, Scol, but I do not think the solution to my restlessness lies here or now. I have you to train first, don't I?'*

'Oh. Yes, Sa,' she replied, though she was still troubled by the subtle thread of discontent that tainted her mentor's Blessing.

When Elys brought his attention back to the driver, Daki's expression was unreadable.

"Are you... did she... is Learza Blessed?" he stuttered out. "I don't get to be around others like me much, but that.. were you two talking?"

Learza sat up, her head held high as she awaited her mentor's response. His pride in her always filled their connection with a deep sense of satisfaction.

"Yes, Daki, she is. While all creatures feel the pull of Tir's Will, very few are actually Blessed. Learza is a unique case. Her Blessing has boosted her intelligence beyond a normal dog's. In her own way, she is quite capable of understanding everything we say to her." Elys reached down and ran his hand over Learza's soft head. "She would not be a Scolyt otherwise."

"Wow," Daki replied, shaking his head with a grin on his face. A moment later, he came out of his reverie and glanced down his watch. "Oh no, look at the time! We'd better get you to the prime minister."

Daki opened the door to his grounder before going around to the other side and getting into the driver's seat. Once everyone was settled, he steered the vehicle out onto the street and accelerated toward a small cluster of buildings visible in the distance. Elys noted as they drew closer that the structures were old and run down, a stark contrast to the clean, bright spaceport they left behind. Remembering the notes on Heronat he read as part of his mission packet, he reflected that the Zemvo's money could have been better spent.

The Zemvo sent aid to Heronat soon after the end of the Ilandu wars, as it did with all planets in the Diot Federation. With the little farming communities fairly self-sufficient, the planetary government used the funds to build the new port in hopes of attracting settlers to the distant outpost. Thus far the efforts to bring in new colonists was failing and the dearth of traffic meant the port retained its sparkle even a century after its construction.

The efficient vehicle made quick time of the distance and the travelers soon arrived in Barun, pulling up to the steps of the capitol. Bidding Daki a fond farewell the two companions found themselves in front of an impressive stone hall. The stairs of the local government's main building were worn down by centuries of footsteps. At the top of the steps, an overhang towered above a metal-trimmed, wooden door, its hinges dingy with age. The handle felt cool and smooth under Elys's grasp, the brass polished to a burnished shine by the repeated touch of human hands.

Inside, the cavernous foyer echoed with the sound of Learza's nails against the marble. Three lifts stood waiting directly across from the entrance. The only furniture was a reception desk off to the side and a few benches along the opposite wall. Elys approached the desk and was greeted by a young woman who smiled and asked their business.

"Fraer Elys Ki Dul and Scolyt Learza to see the prime minister," he told her. "We represent Vostra Heinlein on Zemvo business."

"Oh, yes, of course. Premier Oepon has been expecting you," she explained as she typed their information into the terminal in front of her.

"Would Learza like to stay with me while you meet with him?"

Learza's ears perked up at the mention of her name. *'Sa, I'll stay with her. She's got snacks for me somewhere. I can smell them.'*

Elys laughed, garnering a strange look from the receptionist. *'Okay, Scol, but no begging.'*

He then turned back to the woman. "Learza seems to think there may be food involved if she remains with you. I shouldn't be long, I'm just a courier after all, not a negotiator."

"No problem at all. And yes, I do have something for her

to nibble," the receptionist replied, handing him a pass to attach to his long coat and a keycard for the lift.

A quick lift ride and a walk down a long empty hallway later and Elys was in front of another pair of wooden doors. He knocked softly and a gruff voice answered, "Enter!"

The office inside was conservative in its appointments. Most of the furniture consisted of basic grey steel, the seats cushioned in burnt orange upholstery similar to the inexpensive, but sturdy, blue fabric found throughout the Hantirri monastaries.

Behind the desk that dominated the room sat a middle-aged man, greying at his hairline with a deep furrow in his brow as he concentrated on the screen in front of him.

"You the courier?" he asked without glancing up.

"Yes, sir, I'm Fraer Elys Ki Dul. Vostra Heinlein requested that these papers be brought to you with all haste. I believe they are of some urgent importance." Elys replied, using the formal tone he worked hard to maintain in the presence of diplomats and dignitaries.

"Fraer? They sent a damned Hantirri?" Looking up, the Premier scanned Elys up and down, a frown etched on his face. "Must be important if they had to send some monk to guard it."

"I do not know for sure, Sir. I am but the courier." Elys replied with a quick bow and as much diplomacy as he could muster.

The man squinted at the Hantirri as if he could discern some clue about Elys's intentions through looks alone. "And how do I know you haven't tampered with the message? Hmm?"

A brief wave of frustration passed through Elys's mind before he was able to bank it down and answer the pointed accusation with calm reassurance. "Because it is on paper and well sealed, sir, not on a disc with a vulnerable encryption."

The Prime Minister growled at him in return, doing nothing to hide his dissatisfaction. "Give it here, monk. You'll wait downstairs for my reply."

Elys passed the official the packet of papers, secured in an envelope by an old-fashioned wax seal. "Certainly." he told the premier.

The man grabbed the packet and waved Elys toward the door without a further word.

Upon his return to the lobby, the fraer was pounced on by his scolyt, her concern emanating through their bond. *'Sa, he didn't trust you. He upset you.'*

'You're right, Scol, he didn't trust me, but remember that he is the leader of this planet and deserves our respect just the same.' Elys scruffled Learza's head as she dropped back down on all fours and resumed her usual position at his side. *'Thank you for worrying about me, Learza, but my pride can handle it.'*

He then grinned at the woman behind the desk. "Loads of trouble, was she?"

She laughed in return. "Oh yes, lots of mischief in that one."

'Sa, I was good, honest!' his student replied, full of exaggerated indignance.

Elys's grin grew wider and his mood lightened with the teasing. *'I know, young one, I know.'*

The woman then rose and came out from behind her station. "All set then?"

"Not quite," he replied. "I must wait for the Prime Minister's response."

"Ah, that may take a little while. Can I get you some tea? Perhaps some water for Learza, here?"

'She's nice, Sa.' Learza reassured her mentor, moving over to bump her head against the woman's leg.

Elys smiled at the easy acceptance his student gave to strangers, her instincts proving right more often than not. "Yes, that would be lovely, thank you."

A few moments later, with warm cups in their hands, the two humans watched as Learza enthusiastically lapped up her water.

"You know," the woman spoke, her voice tentative. "Not everyone thinks the Hantirri are untrustworthy. Some people even think they're very important to us all."

She met Elys's eyes, sincerity written across her expression as she put a hand out and squeezed his arm.

Elys nodded his acceptance of her sentiment. He took comfort in the words; it was not often that such feelings were directed towards the Order in this dark time of reformation.

It was almost an hour later, the receptionist back at work and Elys sitting on a nearby bench, when a bespeckled man exited the lift.

"Hantirri. Good, you're still here," his tone was sharp. "Here's the Prime Minister's reply. Well sealed, so mind it doesn't come open."

"I will do my best." Elys replied with a forced, warm smile.

The gesture was lost upon the official, who had already turned his back to hurry toward the lift, slipping between the doors as they closed.

Elys shrugged at the receptionist as he walked toward the door and she rolled her eyes in return.

"Come Learza, what do you say we go home?" The fraer did not have to fake the relieved tone in his voice, it had been many months since the duo had returned to Steeltip Priory, their route taking them on a zigzag course across the galaxy and back.

'Home, Sa? Really home?' Learza's tail began to wag hard, slapping against her mentor's legs.

'Yes, Scol, really home.' Elys laughed, Learza's joyful nature bringing an easy smile to his lips. *'But first, how about a run?'*

'Just try and catch me, Sa!' A wave of love and joy for life washed over the fraer, lifting his spirits as he watched his student dash out the door and into an open field across the quiet street.

Chapter 4
Cult of personality

Ulery Academy of Arts and Sciences, Torant City, Acking

"Attention! Attention, if you would." A loud tapping sound accompanied the voice echoing through the cavernous chamber. In front of a slim steel podium, a tall gangly woman attempted to get the attention of the audience. A few hundred scattered people, deep in their own conversations, covered their ears as the microphone began to feed back.

Under the pressure of the collective glare sent her way, the woman started pressing random buttons on the microphone's controls, her scholar's robes tangling in the cables beneath the podium as the feedback grew to a piercing whine. After a few seconds she threw her hands up in frustration and pulled the curtain aside, yelling for assistance. A pimple-faced student dashed out from behind the drapery and flipped a single switch, cutting off the noise before adjusting the controls to the appropriate volume. Finishing the task with a flourish, he turned to the professor, a smug look on his face. She dismissed him with a disgruntled wave of her hand and he strode back through the curtain, his head held high.

Straightening her disheveled robes and collar, the woman cleared her throat into the microphone. Shying back from it as if it might bite her, she waited until the echo died away. When no further noise erupted from the unit, she approached the podium, still tentative, and again got the attention of the gathered company.

"If you would all take your seats, we are about to begin."

Shuffling sounds and the squeaking of chairs echoed in the lecture hall as talk quieted. A few lingering conversants garnered dirty looks from the woman on the stage until they, too, finished their chatting and took their seats. When all had their focus turned to the front of the auditorium, the woman began her introduction in earnest.

"Thank you for your patience. As some of you may know, I am Dr. Gratika Ward, head of the Department of Social Sciences here at the Academy."

Pausing for a moment, the doctor anticipated at least a smattering of applause following her self-introduction. Still flustered from her technological faux paux, it took a moment for her to realize the room remained silent. Resisting the desire to roll her eyes, she could not help but click her tongue against her teeth before continuing.

"It is with great pleasure that I welcome you all here today." Forcing a pleasant smile onto her face, she gave an extra nod to the members of the press in attendance. "We are honored to present to you one of the leading researchers into the intriguing field of occult studies. Focusing on the practices of the developing tribal societies of the farthest reaches of the Shambles, she has opened up this fledgling field to a wider audience. The data she has uncovered is aiding sociologists in unexpected ways. Her marvelous ability to obtain access to some of the most sequestered people in the galaxy is helping us to understand how our own societies may have developed long ago."

Injecting a false moment of drama into her introduction, Dr. Ward paused again. Her audience simply shifted in their seats, the reporters taking the opportunity to check their notes. Having failed in building any tension in her audience, the doctor rushed headlong into the rest of her introduction.

"Well, I could go on here, but I will let the woman speak for herself. Without any further ado, I present to you, Dr. Asori Kapradina."

Polite applause filled the space as a slim woman appeared from the side of the curtain. She, too, was dressed in scholar's robes, her hair pulled back from her fair face in a simple, albeit tight, hairdo held in place by numerous pins. The combination gave her face a rather severe look, much like one of the tribal masks she was famed for collecting on her travels.

Approaching the platform, she shook Dr. Ward's hand then placed her lecture notes on the podium and turned to face the audience. Preparing to speak, she stopped short when a door at the back of the auditorium slammed open. The gathered company turned to watch a bedraggled man stomp down the aisle and remove his overcoat and scarf before plopping into a seat near the front of the stage. Flashing Dr. Kapradina a quick grin, he rummaged for a moment in his pockets before producing a tattered pad of paper and a pen with a chewed up end.

Noticing he was being watched, the man waved his hand

in a lazy, circular motion at the professor. "Go ahead, Asori, I'm ready now."

Rolling her eyes at the rumpled reporter, the professor cleared her voice before speaking. "Good evening, everyone."

She paused a moment, adjusting the volume on the microphone with a finesse that eluded her colleague. When she continued, her reedy voice carried with clarity across the space.

"I am here to present to you the findings from my latest research trip to Sernpidal. In working with the quiet unassuming Serns, I discovered the depth of meaning in their previously cryptic use of symbology. As you all may know, symbology and sacred texts are my special interest and the Sern sigils have proven especially difficult to decipher. It was two months into my... yes?"

Waving his hand back and forth, high above his head, the latecomer caught her attention. "Dr. Kapradina, I was wondering when you got back from this research trip of yours."

"You were, were you, Regi?" she replied, annoyed by the interruption. "Well, I returned just last week. Though I don't know what that has to do with my lecture..."

He cut her off before she could continue. "So, it's not possible, then, that you were seen in the lower levels, about three weeks ago?" he questioned further, casually scratching his bald head with his stylus.

The professor sighed loud enough for the noise to reverberate through the chamber. "That would be quite impossible, as you well know."

"And you didn't hire a transport to Heronat the next

day?" he pressed her further as people began to shift their attention back and forth between the two of them like spectators at a slamball tournament.

"Why would I want to go to Heronat in the first place, never mind the fact that I was on Sernpidal?" Asori gave a frustrated wave of her hand.

"Could it be that you found your next clue, the next step to bringing you closer to the the secrets of the Ilandu, the secrets left behind by your great-grandfather?" Regi spoke as if stunned that the thought had only just occurred to him, though the professor could see through the exaggerated ruse.

Clenching her hands around the podium's edge, the woman spoke in stilted tones. "That's preposterous. The ancestor you're referring to was a crazed psychopath. It would risk everything I've spent my whole life building to even look into his history. Why would I do that?"

Tapping the pen against his lip, Regi appeared to ponder her comments for a moment. "So, you don't deny that the idea intrigues you. It's just simply too risky for your fragile foothold in the academic world to pursue it?"

Hundreds of eyes swiveled from the reporter to the professor, the spotlight on her all the more striking as the color washed from her face.

"What?" she gasped. Realizing that the other reporters in the room were scribbling down every word, she took a deep breath before speaking. "You know, Regi, you do nothing but follow me around flinging out these wild conspiracies and accusations, all because of my unfortunately dubious heritage. Why?"

Regi grinned, the edges of his yellowy eyes crinkling in mirth. "You've yet to prove me completely wrong here, Asori."

"Don't let him do this to you, milady!" A new voice broke into the verbal duel. Regi turned to face the broad-shouldered young man seated in the front row, now pleading with the professor.

"What was that?" he asked, intrigued by the reaction of this new player in their little game, he craned his neck to see the man better.

Leaping to his feet the man began to shout at the reporter. "You are cruel and evil, treating the mistress as if she were a commoner!"

He jumped onto his chair, waving his arms to emphasize his words. "She will be honored one day! All those who receive the Blessing through her efforts will laud her. And you!" he pointed a finger at Regi, his voice filled with rage as he railed at the man. "You shall find yourself in the gutter!"

Turning to stare at the wild man suddenly in their midst, the audience could do nothing but watch as he stood there, breathing heavily with the effort of his outburst and distress. The look on Dr. Kapradina's face registered her shock at the situation and Regi settled into his seat, smiling like a satisfied tusk cat.

"Well, well, so you are up to something, Asori. Care to elaborate on this young man's claim?"

Recovering from her initial shock, Asori Kapradina swallowed hard and spoke in an emotionless voice. "I have no idea who this disturbed young man is."

"No! No, mistress, you know who I am!" Growing more distraught at her rejection, the man continued to shout as he stepped down from the chair and made his way toward her. "I am the most loyal of your followers. I am of those destined to be Blessed! Do not deny me! Let me take my place at your side!"

Two guards came in through the curtain at a run. Grabbing the agitated man they began to escort him, forcefully, from the room. He fought them the whole way, screaming at the top of his lungs.

"No! No! Tell them, Lady! Tell them! He shall rise! He shall rise! And all shall praise you!"

The door shut behind him, sealing out his screams as an uncomfortable silence fell over the room. A third guard appeared and approached her. They whispered for a moment, the guard covering the microphone to conceal their discussion. He pointed at Regi, but with an insistent shake of the professor's head he shrugged his shoulders and left. Asori Kapradina's hands shook as she lifted a glass from the podium and took a few sips of water. The small comfort gave her a moment to clear her thoughts and when she spoke, her confidence began to return.

"I must apologize for the interruption, my fellow colleagues and students. In the course of my work I have unearthed many occult secrets and this knowledge has lead some people to develop an unhealthy attachment to my work, claiming they are my followers. It is a sad and desperate group who harbors some delusion that I will bring them some kind of power because I am the descendant of a madman," she laughed, shaking her head at the absurdity of the situation. "They are mostly harmless, though at times, as you can see, they can get a little out of hand."

A soft chuckle murmured through the crowd as Asori began to win back her audience. "Now if Mr. Dewenki will be so kind as to refrain from further agitating my little cult, I will continue with this lecture."

When the next wave of laughter settled down, the professor dove back into her presentation, completing it without further interruption.

A few hours later she emerged from the shining concrete and steel building into the blustery evening. Darkness settled its velvety quiet over the landscape, aided by the deep snow that muffled any noise along the wide causeway. Buttoning her coat against the chill, Asori walked along the sidewalk toward home, her boots crunching the salt granules struggling to keep the ice at bay.

Passing a crevice between two of the academy's buildings, a whisper from the shadowed alleyway caught her attention. "Psst. Psst. Milady, over here."

Looking around and seeing no on else on the sidewalk to witness her actions, Asori slipped into the passage. Her eyes adjusting to the light enough for her to take aim, she slapped the figure standing in the gloom.

"You bloody fool!" she berated the man, her words filled with authority and venom. "I should cut you loose right now."

Rubbing his face like a wounded child, the man sniveled, "Lady, please, no!"

"What were you thinking?" she continued, her voice a harsh whisper. "You could have jeopardized everything!"

Stepping closer to her, the man put a hand out as if to touch her sleeve. "I am sorry, milady, but that foul reporter was insulting you. He has caused you so much grief this last year."

Dr. Kapradina clenched her fists, readying to strike him again. Preparing for the onslaught, the man dropped to his knees and bent his head in supplication. A thrill passed through her seeing this man in such a vulnerable position and she held back her hand. Reveling in her power over him, she began to rethink her threat to release him from her service.

Sighing as she relaxed her shoulders, Asori reached down and brought his face up so she could meet his eyes. Any innocence she might have found there had been swept away in the course of the errands he ran for her. All that remained was his loyalty and a quiet heat that burned beneath the sea of cobalt blue. "Yes, he certainly has. Perhaps it is time we removed him from the equation, hmm? We are too close to the ritual to risk being exposed."

Finding the opportunity to return to her good graces, the man smiled and stood up. If he was not to be beaten, then there were other things she desired of him. The chill winter air seemed less cold as his temperature rose. "It shall be taken care of, milady. He shall trouble you no more."

"Good. I want it done tonight," she told him as she allowed him to step closer and begin pulling at the pins binding her hair.

"Ah yes, but first things first, hmm?" she gave him a predatory grin.

Helping her loyal follower to finish his task, Asori pulled

the last pin from her coif and shook her hair loose before pulling him closer. He shivered as she ran her hand down the back of his neck just before she ran her tongue along his jugular.

Biting at his ear as he pulled her closer in his excitement, she whispered, "Remember, my boy, to take care of all the evidence, anything that would trace back to me. Do not fail me."

"Yes, milady. It shall be done," he replied, kissing her with urgency as he pulled her deeper into the shadows.

Chapter 5
Letter of intent

On the road from Barun, Heronat, Morlan Sector

Learza was always happiest when she was able to let her senses run free. The pulse of life thrummed in her very cells, tempting her to follow its call. Soft breezes joined her in play and she raced them across the grassy plain. Appearing from its hutch, a hopping rodent began to run and Learza chased it for a moment until it disappeared down a hole a few yards away. Rolling in the tall grass, the stalks scratching the itches on her back, she soaked in the warm rays of the sun before leaping up to run with the wind once more.

Popping her head out of the waist high grass, she sensed her mentor there, in the center of her orbit where he belonged. His warm presence was a stabilizing force in her life, keeping her focused. He aided her with the discipline of the Hantirri, that she might learn to use her talents to help others. When she was able to ease the suffering of the those around her, the chorus of Tir's Will hummed with even more strength in her soul.

Deep in her heart, she knew what her true purpose was, the person she was there to aid more than any other.

There was a space within Elys that needed to be filled, a void that kept him distant from others as if unwilling to open himself to any but just the right soul. Learza took up residence there when she was a pup, holding that place within his heart until the day someone came to claim it. In taking the dog as his personal scolyt, Elys had set himself even further apart from the other Hantirri, forever changing the course of his destiny. Their first meeting was the beginning of a journey and while she did not know the destination, nor how long it would take, Learza knew her presence kept him on his path.

Elys Ki Dul watched his scolyt run in widening circles around him as he walked at a leisurely pace toward the spaceport, enjoying the warm sun and clean, clear air. Joy crested over him in waves as she flew across the ground, reveling in her freedom as she set a hard pace for herself. He smiled, soaking in her bliss along with the warm sunshine. Turning his thoughts inward, he began to reflect on the unique perspective he gained as her mentor.

Almost five years had passed since their fateful meeting. In all that time, he had yet to regret his decision, though it was a rougher road than he had ever imagined for himself. It made him chuckle now when he thought of his younger self, a quiet, unassuming fraer, approaching the Grand Synod and informing them that not only should Learza be a member of the order, but that he should personally oversee her training.

Never before had Elys found himself at odds with that august body, but that day he shocked even himself as he vehemently argued for Learza's acceptance into the order.

Initiates were taught in groups by tradition, and it had been centuries since there was a dedicated pairing of fraer and scolyt. Noting the singularity of Learza's existence, the Synod was reluctant to further isolate her from the other initiates. Still, knowing the young fraer to be one of the most reserved and humble of their brethren gave the Synod pause and, after much reflection, they eventually relented to his request.

His bright smile fading, Elys reflected on the delicate balance the Hanitirri struggled to maintain. Besides the public's loss of faith in Tir, many people still looked over their shoulders when the Hantirri were around, fearing that each fraer may be the harbinger of a coup. It made the order's renewed position as messengers, healers and clergy all the more tenuous, despite the very public disarmament and reaffirmation of their fealty to the Zemvo over a century ago. Taking some solace in the continuing peace, Elys was relieved that the Ilandu seemed to have been fully eradicated, slowly fading into the realm of myth and nightmare. There was enough evil-doing among the pirates, smugglers and thieves of the galaxy without the threat of the Cursed hanging over their heads.

Looking up from his reverie, Elys found he had wandered quite far along the road. The spaceport loomed before him, sunlight glistening off its surface as waves of heat rose from the tarmac surrounding the monument to ill-spent funds. Elys whistled sharply between his teeth and, a few moments later, Learza returned to his side. She was panting heavily, her tail wagging so hard Elys thought it might dislodge from her body.

'Hello, Sa! Did you see that hopper? Did you listen to the wind?' The voice was warm against his mind.

'Yes, young one, I did. Did you enjoy yourself?' Crouching next to his excited scolyt, Elys checked her feet for cuts.

'Yes, sir. I wish we could stay. The sun is warm here.' Learza wiggled as he continued his inspection, picking stray blades of grass from her coat and pulling a small bug out of her ear.

'I know, Scol. And right now Torant is under heavy snow, so I'm glad you've soaked it all in.' Satisfied that his apprentice was clean and healthy, Elys scruffled her ears as he stood up. *'Come, we've a long journey home.'*

'Snow? I like snow, too, Sa! Let's go!' Learza gave a joyful jump into the air, but when she came back down, she stopped in her tracks. Elys, too, froze in place.

'Sa?' she began sniffing the air, taking in any information she could through her physical senses.

'Yes, Learza, I sense it, too. Someone is looking for us.' Of all the varied gifts granted to the Blessed, only one was given to all of them. Scanning the area around them, Elys felt for the telltale ripples originating from one of his brethren.

The person was not outside of the terminal. Stretching his senses further, the faint disruption clarified in his mind's eye into a single point of light moving erratically inside the cavernous terminal.

'Can we go find them, Sa? They need help.' Learza released a low whine, originating deep in her chest.

Reassuring her with a pat on the head, Elys agreed with her. *'Yes, let's see what we can do.'*

Taking off at a quick jog, they arrived at the entrance

to the port within moments and there they paused. While never truly crowded, even on the busiest of days, there were enough people milling around the terminal to muddle Elys' focus.

Elys closed his eyes, blocking out the crowd and fixing on the elusive rippling energy. He got a fix just as Learza honed her own senses toward their target. Elys had long ago acknowledged that his student's ability to hear the song of Tir's Will was deeper and more powerful than his own. He rarely hesitated to depend on her when the situation called for it. Her more immediate connection to the present and vital energy of all life allowed the scolyt to locate the distraught Blessed before her mentor and she took off toward a gate at the far end of the terminal.

Opening his eyes, the small grin of satisfaction at his scolyt's efficiency faded to a slack-jawed stare as Elys watched Learza dive between passengers and leap over bags with expert ease. He began to hurry after her, dodging those in his path and excusing himself multiple times as he caught their muttered comments.

"Crazy monk, where'd he get that dog anyway. No right to be havin' animals, probably don't treat her right."

"Aww, they're playing tag. How sweet. So nice to see a young man with a dog. What? He's Hantirri? Oh, well, he seemed nice anyway. Guess you can't always judge by looks, can you?"

Elys watched in horror as Learza jumped up and put her paws on the shoulders of a young woman in loose blue robes. He could tell the canine was being friendly, but the girl was obviously clueless in the face of a strange animal who appeared out of nowhere. Straightening his clothing with a quick tug, Elys approached them, a forced smile on his face.

"Learza, down now, let her catch her breath," he spoke, his tone sharp that the girl might see he was in control of the situation.

'Sorry, Sa! Look! I found her!' Circling the girl, Learza herded her closer to Elys with each nudge. The color in the girl's face washed away, her hands up in a defensive posture, unsure of what the animal at her back was trying to accomplish.

'I see that, Scol, but you should not have jumped on her.' he chided. Despite her wonderful, open heart, Learza had a tendency to forget that her affection could be misconstrued by the unsuspecting folk she targeted with her enthusiasm.

'I didn't mean to scare her, Sa.' Learza's voice was conciliatory and she started nuzzling the girl's hand in effort to make amends. The girl took a step back and Learza, calmer now having been reminded of her position, returned to Elys' side and sat next to him.

"My apologies for my scolyt's brashness," he said with a quick bow. "She was overexcited and has been reprimanded for her loss of control." Elys tried smiling at the girl, but knowing little else to say to ease her fears any further, he cleared his throat and continued. "Now that we have found you, why were you so desperate to find us?"

The girl was still wary, her hands shaking. Standing there stunned, she did not utter a word until she spotted the mark on Elys' forehead and the base of his throat.

"You are of the Wandering Brethren?" she hazarded

a guess, the desire to complete her mission as quickly as possible overcoming her timidity. The safety of her cloister felt light years away as she stood here with the stranger and his dog. If these were the ones she sought, then she might return to her seclusion in peace.

"If you mean the Hantirri, then yes, we are," he replied with another bow as he reached a hand down to Learza's head, including her in the introduction.

Looking at the dog, the girl noticed the crystal around her neck, acceptance and understanding reaching her mind, then answered the fraer's bow with a small smile and a nod of her own. "I am Vanta Dimsdale, of the Tirtet. I am so glad I found you before you departed. I have an urgent message from the Abbot."

She passed Elys a scroll of paper, bound with a blue ribbon. He hesitated for a moment, but with a quick nod of acknowledgment from the girl, he untied the binding and unrolled the scroll. Scanning the information, his heart rate increased as the contents sunk in, and he looked up at the girl for confirmation before returning his attention to the letter.

'Sa, will you read it to me?' came the curious nudge on his mind.

It took a moment before he was able to reply, at a loss as to what to do with the knowledge he just received. Shaking off the spectre of dread from his mind, he finally told her *'Yes, Learza, of course. It says:*

> *To the Wandering Brethren,*
> *The diary of Aedan Kapradina has been forcibly*

stolen from our possession. We safeguarded it to best of our abilities and three of our number have been returned to the Void in its defense. The information that book contains has been unleashed upon the galaxy once again. As the Grand Synod well knows, this could be the final key that would lead to the resurrection of those whom your order so recently sent into defeat.

The burden has been removed from our possession and it is up to you to do with this information as you will. The Tirtet have completed their final task on behalf of the Wandering Brethren and until the time you return to the true path of Tir's Will, we shall speak no more.

Pass this vital information on to the Wise One called Grannie Hella. Her last known residence was somewhere near your enclave on Acking. Take heart and find her, for she is well versed in such matters and will know what to do.

Tir's Blessing upon you all,
Abbot Yevian Emerick'

The two Hantirri looked at each other for a moment, letting the very idea that the Ilandu could be risen from the ashes of their destruction process in their minds. It had been over one hundred years since the defeat of the last Ilandu leader, his army cornered on Vestra. When the dust cleared he was declared dead, his body interred in a mass grave along with his followers rather than given proper rites. There had not been a shadow of threat from that day forward, until this letter came into Elys's possession.

'*The synod needs to hear this,*' Learza's statement was decisive, she sat up straighter as if the action backed up her resolution.

Elys agreed with ready confirmation. '*Yes, Scol, they most certainly do. We're leaving on the next transport.*'

Looking up, Elys found the girl was gone. Apparently the final task of the insular Tirtet was the delivery of this note and she felt no need to make sure something would be done about it. He could not imagine removing himself so far from galactic goings on as to be unconcerned with the return of the Ilandu; perhaps there was not something here for him after all. Slipping the parchment into a pocket on Learza's vest, with a cleansing breath he let his frustration and discontent slide away. His search for fulfillment would have to wait once more.

Making their way back through the terminal, Elys approached the ticket desk near the main gate. A short argument ensued and he was forced to produce his own Zemvo credentials as well as Learza's before the middle aged man behind the counter relented, moving passengers off the next flight to make room for them. By the time their paperwork was straightened out, the duo had to run through the terminal once again, just making it onto the shuttlecraft before the doors were sealed shut.

The short flight to the larger transport orbiting the planet gave them little time to think. At last, arriving in their cramped cabin, the two Hantirri began to settle in for the journey. After rearranging the few items of furniture to make space for Learza to move about easier, Elys removed his coat and sat on the bed next to her. Releasing the clasps on her vest, he helped Learza wiggle out of the garment and she jumped down to roll about on the floor for a minute.

'*Not exactly the way we would have liked to be going home, is it, Scol?*' Elys asked, removing his boots and stretching his toes.

All her itches satisfied, Learza jumped back onto the bed and, curling up on a blanket at its foot, gave a wide, noisy yawn. '*No, but maybe we'll get a real mission out of this, Sa.*'

Scrubbing his hands over his scalp, disheveling his cropped hair so it stuck out in all directions, Elys sighed at his scolyt's enthusiasm, reminding her, '*A fraer does not look for more than he is given, young one.*'

'*But we could handle it, Sa. You're the best and I can do things my way.*' she argued, defensive of their abilities.

Shaking his head, he argued back, '*I appreciate your faith, Learza, but I am not the man suited to those missions. I accept the Will of Tir, but I do not foresee any great deeds in my future, nor do I look for them.*'

'*You underestimate yourself, Sa,*' she moved over and put her head in his lap.

Scratching behind her ears, he corrected her with a firm tone, '*No, young one, I simply understand my limitations and accept that there are others better suited to those tasks.*'

'*You could do it, if you wanted to, Sa,*' she picked her head up, regretting the words instantly, for she knew she spoke without thinking.

Removing his hand from her head, he gave her a nudge toward the footboard. '*That is enough, Learza. It is not our mission and I will hear no more about it. Now I'd like to get some rest and you should as well. We've had a long day and when we return to Acking we must be ready to meet with the Grand Synod.'*

'Yes, Sa.' A sense of submission and a wave of apology flowed to Elys through their bond as Learza curled her tail between her legs before settling on the blanket, her head on her paws.

'We are not here for great things nor glory, Learza. We must simply serve the Will of Tir.' Accepting her apologetic energy, he returned it with a soft nudge of peace before closing his eyes and releasing the trials of the day into the Void.

Chapter 6
No place like home

Public Transport Sky Lanes, Torant City, Acking

Sitting aboard the shuttlecraft, Elys watched the sun creep towards the horizon, shining with a dim light onto the city below. Snow encrusted every horizontal surface and the tops of many of the space-scraping buildings disappeared into the scattered clouds above.

Learza stood on her seat when the outline of Steeltip Enclave came into view, craning her neck to look out the front viewport and wagging her tail, thwacking it against the closest wall in anticipation. After months of travel, home was within sight, bringing a comfort that pushed aside some of the icy thoughts recent events brought to her mind. Her enthusiasm garnered a few chuckles from her fellow Hantirri aboard the shuttle, one commenting that she agreed with Learza's tail completely.

Setting down among a few other craft in front of the gargantuan structure, their shuttle opened its doors, releasing its cargo of ascetics into the cold. Elys stopped for a moment outside the craft, wrapping his coat tighter around him to ward off the chill as he looked up. A passing cloud hid the center spire of the enclave, but many of the upper floors could still be seen. Construction had begun on an upper landing platform that would allow access to the Grand Synod's chambers and some of the other administrative offices of the order. Officially meant to relieve important visitors from the burden of traveling through the labyrinthine halls of the enclave, it was rumored that the structure's true purpose was more covert. Insisted upon by the Zemvo, the platform opened up a vulnerability in the enclaves's defenses that gave the populace a sense of security. It was one of many sacrifices the order allowed to occur as they rebuilt the trust of the populace of the Diot and its ruling body.

With his fellow passengers already making their way into the building, Elys took a deep breath and let go of the small knot of anxiety settling in his chest. Yes, this was home, the best he had found thus far, but he found he was often more restless here than when on a mission. Even the reassurance that he was entrusted with Learza's training brought little comfort when he was faced with the assembled spectrum of powerful Blessed within the edifice sitting before him.

Sensing the agitation in his reverie Learza leaned against him, her attempt to comfort his unspoken concerns bringing him back to the present. Releasing the dark thoughts and fears, Elys reached to the peace he found within their bond and smiled at his companion.

'Well, we're home, Scol.' He placed a hand on her soft head, resting it there as she turned to nuzzle it with her nose.

'Yes, Sa. It will be nice to sleep someplace quiet tonight.'

He chuckled. *'That's right. No rumbling engines to disturb you for a little while.'*

Climbing the stone steps, they passed by the towering statues guarding the entrance. These representations of great Hantirri of the past were meant to serve as inspiration to those of the present. Somehow, Elys always felt that these sentinels looked down upon him, searching out his weaknesses. He felt sure one day they would slam the doors shut in his face instead of welcoming him with open arms.

Learza urged him forward, anxious to get inside and see what had changed since their most recent departure. Nodding greetings to fraers passing them on the way, the duo walked through the arching doorway and into the cavernous entrance hall of the enclave. Once inside, the deep blue carpeting, unchanging in its solidity, was a reinforcing signal of home for both of them. Learza walked ahead of her mentor, sniffing the ground in front of her, soaking in the familiar smells.

Elys looked around, searching for friendly faces and recognized only one of the many people moving through the vast space. The man was well known to all, as was the strength of his Blessing. The bright, shining star of the order, Anos Keener. Kind and giving, he was the best the order had to offer, and his presence only served to increase Elys' self-consciousness. The slight tightness in his chest at the sight of the other fraers gathered around Anos was loosened when he noticed a petite woman approaching him. She smiled at him, a warm glint in her eye.

"Fraer Ki Dul, greetings." Bowing her head, she looked down at Learza.

"Fraer Tan, it is good to see you." Elys straightened his posture a little. "This is Learza, my scolyt."

When the elder Hantirri hesitated in greeting her, Learza took point, as she often did in such situations, and bowed her head. Hepsi Tan smiled and bowed in return.

"Scolyt Learza. It is a true pleasure to meet the you." Kneeling down, she met Learza's eyes and the scolyt approached her, nudging her outstretched hand. Learza sniffed it for a moment before moving in to give the fraer a quick lick on her cheek. The woman laughed.

"How are you, Sa?" Elys asked as she stood back up, wiping her damp cheek.

"Oh, I am just fine. Tir's Will continues to gift me with good health and smooth waters," she replied with a knowing smile before returning her attention to the young scolyt at her feet, looking directly at her as she continued. "Learza, would you be so kind as to excuse us for a few moments?"

Learza looked to Elys, unwilling to leave his side. *'Sa?'*

"It's alright, Learza, we just need to speak for a few moments. All is well between us, do not worry," he responded with a wave of comforting energy.

'Yes, Sa,' she replied before turning to explore the far side of the cavernous room.

Once she was gone, Hepsi Tan focused her attention on the young man she considered a favorite, giving him a quick once over of his physical condition before probing into his emotional status.

"And how is it with you, my most woebegone scolyt?" she asked, sincere concern in her voice. "I am sorry I was out of touch when you took on Learza. I would have liked to meet her before this."

"I am well, Sa. Learza is a joy to train, so intelligent and she's been gifted with such an amazing Blessing, it far outstrips my own." He smiled, watching as his charge disappeared behind a tall pillar, her excitement at some new discovery flickering through their bond.

"Hmm. Yes, she is a special case. Still, it is most unusual and I wonder if this does not further alienate you from your brethren, myself included?" She pressed him to elaborate, sure he would remain as reticent as ever, but hopeful that taking on the challenge of Learza's training had loosened him up a little.

Elys shrugged his shoulders. "It may be so, but I follow the Will of Tir. None of us are on an easy path and I hold to the hope that I may yet find the purpose for my inner discontent."

Memories of long discussions flickered through the elder fraer's mind as they spoke. Always willing to talk about any problems the young man was facing, Fraer Tan did her best to keep the often moody, young Elys on track. Soon after he arrived at the enclave, she found that the child in her care responded much better to encouragement than hard discipline. At times wondering if she did him a disservice by not toughening him up better, he still flourished considerably well under her tutelage. Despite the subtle nature of his Blessing - for there were many more powerful than he - when the time came she had no reservations about him taking his vows.

They stood talking for a few more minutes before Elys

begged her pardon. "If you will excuse me, Sa, I have an appointment with the Synod on some urgent news."

She squeezed his arm. "Yes, of course." She held his gaze for a moment, searching for some elusive sign. "Elys, you know if ever you wish, you may still come and speak with me."

"Thank you, Sa. I may yet someday have need." Bowing his head to her, she returned the gesture, then departed.

"Learza?" Unable to see his charge, Elys sent the query through their bond. *'Scol?'*

'Coming, Sa!' came the reply and, once she was by his side, they began making their way up the grand stairs leading to the bank of lifts that would take them to the upper floors of the enclave.

Many stops later, at times crushed to the back of the tight space as Hantirri boarded and departed from the lift, they arrived outside of the Synod chamber. The harried acolytes acting as receptionists that day took their reply from Premier Oepon, passing it to another of the Hantirri couriers who would, in turn, deliver it to the Zemvo. The main focus of their primary mission complete, they took a seat on the cushioned bench along the far wall of the reception area.

Their wait passed in no time at all, the Synod having a full docket that day and keeping as close to their tight schedule as possible. Before long the towering wooden doors opened and a few fraers departed, whispering to each other as Elys and Learza were escorted inside.

Windows that allowed a one hundred and eighty degree view of the city let in the late afternoon light, the wintry sun gleaming off the great Ternbal Sea in the distance as well as the ceaseless lines of air traffic close by. The eyes of the Synod were upon Elys as he stepped forward, the attention causing his chest to tighten before a slow breath allowed him to speak.

"Greetings, your Graces," Elys opened the dialogue.

A dozen heads nodded their greeting in return.

"We understand you have most urgent news for us. As you are arriving from Heronat, we are curious what could be so important," Mika Ashbaugh, the most senior member of the Synod, addressed them.

"Here, your Graces." Elys produced the scroll from a pocket on Learza's vest.

One of the mikas read the letter out to the others. While she did so, Elys fiddled with a small loose thread along his cuff. Sensing Learza watching his fingers instead of keeping her attention on the proceedings, he stopped the action and guided her focus back to the Synod. When the letter was finished Mika Ashbaugh nodded to the other members and spoke.

"I am sure I can speak for the rest of the Synod here. I understand your worry at receiving this information, Fraer Ki Dul. It is a disturbing development. Unfortunately, it is but a seed of a rumor and there is little we can do about it except monitor the situation."

Thoughts fluttered through Elys' mind. This was a threat of the return of the Ilandu, did they mean to do nothing? Surprised confusion evident in his voice, he told them, "I'm not sure I understand, your Grace."

Mika Cowert, a man with silvery grey hairs beginning

to show among his otherwise dark hair, explained, "Well, as you know, the Hantirri order is in a precarious position within the Diot. Many would like to see us removed from our service to the Zemvo and some would prefer to see us disbanded entirely. To bring up a possible threat of an Ilandu resurrection now would make us appear as warmongers and rabble rousers, playing on the fears of the populace in order to regain power. This would only serve to aid those who wish to see us completely annihilated."

"So we will do nothing?" The thought of ignoring the dangerous information he had just presented to them still did not make sense in Elys' mind. The Grand Synod was rarely wrong in such matters, doing their best to protect the order and the Diot, but there was a nagging feeling within his heart that something here was very wrong.

"Had you heard of the Kapradina Diary before receiving this information?" Mika Ashbaugh questioned him, her tone taking on a hint of condescension that set Elys's doubts swirling once again.

"No, I had not," he admitted, wishing now he had taken the time to research the matter first.

Ashbaugh nodded and continued her explanation. "It is a small collection of apocryphal knowledge, supposedly holding some information that could lead to the raising of the dead. This task is impossible, none return from the Void unless Tir wills it so. The information in that diary, while potentially dangerous from a political standpoint, poses little true threat."

A slight flush of blood rising to his face, Elys asked his next question, dreading the answer though he expected its outcome. "And what of this Grannie Hella?"

Ashbaugh shook her head in a subtle motion. Elys was unsure if the disappointment was directed at him or not, but took it as an admonishment just the same. "She is a fable, Fraer Ki Dul, supposedly a being of great power. But the idea of a mythological being taking up residence in the lower levels of Torant City seems rather unlikely."

"I see. I am sorry, your Graces. I seem to have been played for a fool." The loose thread in his cuff had become all the more interesting over the last few minutes and, hidden beneath his sleeve, he began to worry at it, testing its strength and measuring it against his fingers.

Realizing she had put the younger man on edge, Ashbaugh attempted to correct the situation. "No, Elys. You did as you thought necessary and we will need to monitor the situation for any further developments. It is also sad, but important news that the Tirtet have cut the final tie that kept us bound to each other. While we may disagree on ideology, they are still our brother Blessed and this rift is a sad wound upon our history."

"Yes, your Grace." Knowing the revered Synod member was trying to soften the blow did little to ease Elys' mind, though he now had little to fear of an Ilandu resurrection. Resolving to do some research on the order's lore while he was in residence, his mind was drawn back into the present moment when Mika Ashbaugh shifted the discussion to he and Learza.

"Now then, as for you and your scolyt here," the mika began.

An inner flicker of self doubt surfaced again in Elys'

heart. While the woman's tone betrayed no reprimand, still he had no thought as to what the other's next words might be. Too often for his own comfort, Elys' imagination would run off with him and he would envision the Synod separating him from Learza or expelling them both from the order for some error and he wondered if this would be that time.

Reaching out for their bond, a strong source of comfort in such times, he found Learza's attention seemed to have wandered off, only now at the mention of her title was she bringing it back into focus. The lapse brought his own thoughts snapping back to the present as he felt the weight of his responsibility settle firmly on his shoulders once more. He was a fraer with his own scolyt, a Hantirri trained, not one to allow petty fears and insecurities get the better of his mind.

"Yes, your Grace?" he replied, swallowing his fears to ensure his voice held no timidity.

The senior mika continued, a small grin of pride now surfacing on her face. "We are pleased with the work you have done for the Zemvo. There have been no complaints about either of your conduct and all packages arrived safely and securely at their destinations."

Relief at last swept through Elys' mind. "Thank you. We do our best to represent the order as both efficient and trustworthy."

Mika Cowert spoke now, agreeing with the sentiment, "And this you have done. Yet it has been more than half a year since you have returned to the enclave and a Hantirri is not meant to be naught but a beast of burden for the

Zemvo. There is training your scolyt has yet to complete and a Hantirri needs to spend time reflecting upon their path and the Will of Tir."

With a nod of understanding, Elys awaited what news the mika would present to him next. Were they to be assigned a more critical task? Learza was not yet ready to take on one of the more dangerous missions, her mind still too prone to distraction. *'As is my own,'* he chided himself.

The mika continued, "As such, we have chosen to put you on sabbatical. When you deem you are prepared to return to duty, you will present yourself before us. Until then, may Tir's Blessing be upon you both."

A knot of nerves loosened at the back of Elys' neck. They would be able to rest and develop Learza's skills without interruption. It was a wonderful gift and it opened up a world of possibilities to them. "Thank you, your Graces."

Turning to leave, a thought popped into his head unbidden. Learza, sensing him struggling with a question, prodded at his mind.

'What are you thinking, Sa?'

He shook her off, *'It is a minor thing, Scol, do not trouble yourself. Come, let's go get something to eat and return to our quarters.'*

Chapter 7
What dreams may come

Steeltip Enclave, Torant City, Acking

The dining hall of the enclave was always busy. With fraers arriving at all hours and keeping such varied schedules, even in the late evening folk could be found clustered around tables chatting with one another over their meals. His thoughts focused on his meeting with the Synod and the lingering sense of something out of place left Elys with little desire to socialize. Putting in a request for a few things to stock their kitchen took only a few moments and, with a piece of fruit in hand, he and his scolyt were soon headed up to their quarters.

Vows of poverty left little chance of theft within the enclave. As such none of the doors locked, allowing Elys to simply lift the latch of the humble wooden door. Stepping into the rooms he and Learza called their own, the faint scent of cleaning solution greeted him, the fading light of day shone through the window, freshly washed and dominating the space. A few cushions sat neatly stacked against one unadorned wall and a firmly-cushioned, blue couch was along the other, a low table between them. Off to the right side of the entrance was a doorway leading to sleeping quarters and directly to the left there was a galley kitchen with two chairs set under the work surface.

The efficiency of the delivery system in the enclave meant that as Elys finished changing into his traditional robes, there was a knock on the door. After taking the box from a young acolyte he set about unpacking the containers and preparing their meal. Relaxing into the task at hand, his troubled thoughts were pushed to the side as he worked. Learza sat on one of the chairs, watching with rapt attention as he chopped vegetables and set them to cooking in a pan. Sniffing at the wet, white block he set on the cutting board next, she turned up her nose at the strange smell.

Laughing, Elys rubbed her head. "That's not for you, young one. That's my dinner."

Reaching into the delivery box one last time, he pulled a package out with a flourish. "This, my scolyt, is yours."

A silent camaraderie fell over the two as they ate their meal in the peace and quiet of their own rooms. When both had finished, Elys cleaned the dishes, still absorbing the freedom of being at home. Once that task was completed, he set out the cushions on the floor before the window and he and Learza took their places for an evening of quiet meditation.

Closing his eyes, Elys mumured the traditional chant of the evening prayer. He soon felt the familiar swirling eddies of power as the Void enveloped them. Guiding Learza through the meditation, Elys spent much of the exercise focused on keeping his wandering scolyt on track. Her easy connection to Tir's Will and the energies gifted to the Blessed allowed her to roam about with ease, following the currents of the Void wherever they might lead. The young dog spent as much time exploring the edges of her perception as she did honing in on the places her mentor guided her.

When at last she accomplished the tasks set out for her, Learza remained enveloped in the peaceful energy of the Void, playing with the tendrils of the bond she shared with Elys. Sensing an unease coming from his end of their tether, she prodded him until he opened his eyes.

'Sa? Something is bothering you.' Standing from her own cushion, Learza moved to Elys' side and waited until he made room for her on his cushion.

'Very perceptive, Scol. I have it shielded from you, yet you have found me out.' He smiled at her as he unbuckled the vest she wore. *'Remember this when we sit down to meditate tomorrow. These are the kind of skills I want to see you develop more fully.'*

'Yes, Sa,' she replied, then hesitantly prodded further. *'Do you need to talk, Sa?'*

'Not yet, Learza. Maybe in the morning. I'd like to think a bit more.' Giving her coat a quick rubdown with his hands, Elys began to yawn. *'Why don't you head off to bed. I'll be there shortly.'*

'Yes, Sa.' She rose and, giving his shoulder a quick nudge with her head, left him for the bedroom.

Elys closed his eyes once more. There was something more he needed to see, he could feel ripples in the Void, but they were in the far distance. Relaxing his body as best he could, he followed a few of the many threads of possibility laid out before him. With foresight never his strongest skill, his focus soon turned to frustration. Try as he might, the elusive threads of clarity remained just out of reach, leaving behind the questions that still worried at his mind. Succumbing to the futility of his search and the weariness in his bones, he stopped his meditation, retiring to his room for much needed rest.

Although falling asleep with ease, Elys slept in disturbed fits and starts, waking often throughout the night. Twisting his sheets around himself, he would awake, fighting against the cotton tethers as he cleared his foggy mind. Each time he opened his eyes he would contain his wild thoughts, focus on the Void, and release his frustrations into its ready embrace. At last, much closer to morning than he desired, he fell into a deeper sleep and began to dream.

Walking along a dark passage carved from stone, he was insubstantial, his own hands a ghostly vapor before his eyes. A door was open at the end of the corridor, flickering light emanating from within the room beyond, drawing him towards it. Entering the room, he was bathed in a red light, its source undetectable, seeming to come from everywhere at once. A voice chanted unfamiliar words, the urgency in its tone growing from a quiet whisper into a screaming, rabid desperation. A sense of deep anger and hatred soaked every surface of the room as power washed over him in a tidal wave of energy.

Forcing himself out of the dream, Elys sat up straight in bed, flinging the covers off and throwing his legs over the side as he gasped for breath. Damp with sweat, he rose and stumbled to the washroom. Splashing his face in cool water cleared his head, though the nightmare still lingered as an oppressive weight on his mind, adding to the thoughts still circling there from the previous day. Giving up on getting back to sleep, he wandered to the main living area and looked out over the skyline. The palest hint of dawn tinted the sky a deep purple and he could almost see the chill in the air.

There was a stirring in the next room and a moment later Learza appeared at his side. She sat looking up at him for a long moment. When he did not react to her presence, she butted him with her head and whined low in her throat. His disturbed thoughts blocking their connection, she was forced to use physical contact to show her concern and drag his focus back to the present. Realizing that he was shutting her out, Elys chastised himself for the lapse in focus and gave his scolyt his full attention. When he did so, he was finally able to receive her thoughts and the wave of concern that flowed from her.

'Sa?' She was distressed at the static in their bond. Kneeling before her, Elys took her head in both his hands and scrubbed at her face before ruffling then smoothing her fur all the way down to her tail. The physical attention always calmed his charge when their bond became frayed, and he frowned at the realization. It happened far too often if the action was second nature to him.

When the task was done, he patted her back, his thoughts still threatening to wander off despite the grounding influence the action gave him. *'Learza. Let's go for a walk, shall we?'*

'Yes, Sa,' she replied in a more relaxed tone, Elys's attention providing the balm that would calm his charge

until he could explain himself better.

Throwing a loose tunic over his sleep pants, Elys didn't bothering dressing any further, his need to move outweighing any sense of propriety. Padding barefoot down one of the many long corridors that divided the enclave, he was pleased to find they were alone. Learza followed him in silence, accustomed to his wanderings with a destination only reached in his heart and mind. On and on they walked, soon rambling through passageways Learza had never seen before. They never took a lift, yet somehow they climbed higher and higher within the structure. At last they walked along a great causeway bordered by grand pillars on one side and immense sheets of glass on the other and Learza could see they were high above the city, the morning light shifting now from purple to many shades of red as the sun began to rise.

'*Scol,*' Elys broke his long silence with an abrupt statement. '*There is a thought that plagues me.*'

'*Yes, Sa?*' She sent a small nudge through their bond, urging him to speak further.

He hesitated for a brief moment before continuing, now beginning to think the question foolish if he were disturbing his scolyt over nothing. But no, the thoughts would not go away and with only one way to resolve them he would need Learza's full cooperation to proceed.

'*Why did Mika Ashbaugh say that Grannie was in the lower levels? The letter said near the enclave. It did not mention where near the enclave.*'

'*Sa! I thought that, too! I didn't think I listened right,*' Learza admitted, the thought coming through with a tinge of self doubt Elys recognized all too well from his own musings.

Elys stopped in his tracks, blurting his reaction out loud. "Learza, I thought your mind was wandering during the discussion! I'm very proud of you."

'Thank you, Sa,' she replied, then began to press him further. *'But what does that mean? Did the Grand Synod lie to us? Why would they do that?'*

Turning to face her, Elys pondered the question for a moment, crossing his arms over his chest. *'I do not think they told us nothing but falsehoods, Scol. I believe their intent is true and they were forthright about their concerns for the order's place in the federation. I think they do not see that letter as a warning sign, but simply another of many situations to monitor.'*

Neither said anything for a few moments, letting the weight of the conversation sit between them while each reached out to the Void, praying for Tir's Will to give them guidance. Learza cocked her head to the side, as if attuning her physical senses would enable her to hear the currents of change with more clarity.

'We are free to do as we please now, Sa?' she asked, the seemingly innocent question carrying none of the joy such freedom should carry.

Elys, sensing where her line of questioning would take them, breathed deeply for a moment. They would plunge forward to follow where the Will of Tir was leading them, though the path was little clearer now than it had been the evening before. *'Yes, Scol. Why? What would you like to do?'*

'Find Grannie Hella,' she put the thought forth, her tone

betraying a hesitance she shared with her mentor about where the journey might end.

Moving to the window, Elys looked down to the lowest areas still visible from their height. Something was rippling through the Void, deep and powerful. He could not pinpoint it, but when combined with his dream it gave him a deep sense of unease. If it were more than a dream, if it was a vision, what then? A whisper in his mind told him there may be something he and Learza could do to change the course of events and avoid the horrific outcome the dream foretold, though he knew in his heart neither of them would come through the experience unchanged.

Learza came to his side, putting her paws up on the railing, that she might look down as well. Sensing the changes in the Void, she wondered if this was the shift that she sought. Was this the thing that would let her mentor fill the empty place in his heart? And if it was, where would she go when its rightful owner appeared to take that place? Pushing the sad thought aside, Learza looked up at Elys and saw a small smile creeping across his face.

"Scol, let us go and dress. There may be a myth hidden in the lower levels. I mean to find her."

Chapter 8
A spell cast in feathered wings

Minner Towers, Torant City, Acking

Snow swirled past a window high above the streets of Torant City. While not one of the most posh addresses in the academic district, the building maintained a subtle elegance that catered to the conservative tastes of the professors from the venerable Ulery Academy.

Watching as the flakes flowed with the whim of the air currents, Asori Kapradina rubbed her bare arms, a chill sliding down her back despite the comfortable temperature inside her apartment. Reaching over to a nearby chair, she pulled a thin sweater over her dress and returned to observing the snow, lost in musings over the journey that lay ahead of her.

"Ah, if only I were going somewhere warm." She spoke to no one in particular, voicing her thoughts aloud as one does who is accustomed to living alone. "Grandfather," she sighed. "Why did you have to get yourself buried somewhere with a winter just as cold as Acking's?"

The quiet sound of delicate gears engaging turned her attention back to the inside of the apartment. An aging android approached her with a tray, his pewter-colored casing gleaming dimly in the soft light.

"Your tea, Dr. Kapradina." The android's voice processor crackled as he spoke.

"Thank you, Javes," Asori replied, taking the mug of tea, skillfully steeped to the perfect sipping temperature. "Will you be sure to keep a pot warm for the rest of the evening? I've much to do before I leave."

The robot paused for a moment before answering. "It will be done, Dr. Kapradina."

"Dismissed," Asori ordered the machine, who stayed frozen for another moment before turning away to comply.

"Must get his processor checked when I return," she reminded herself, shaking her head at her lapse in his upkeep.

The upcoming events continued to distract her from the mundane tasks of daily life. There was never a question of upgrading to a newer model though, despite the rate Javes' gears and circuits were deteriorating. Repairs would be done as needed, for the android would not be decommissioned. He had been a gift from her father when she was but a child.

Looking at the bed, Asori let out a sigh. Bags lay splayed out, a few piles of clothing alongside them. Closet doors sat open, hangers dangling over the edge. Packing clothes was not her forte and her wandering thoughts would not make the chore any easier.

Deciding to move on to a task to which she was better suited, she walked out of the room and down the short hall to her study. Sliding her palm across a panel inside the door upon entering, a series of spotlights set into the ceiling lit the room in a warm, gentle light. Comfortable chairs sat upon an intricately-patterned rug, a table piled with books dominating the center of the space. Filling one wall was the collection of masks she was so famed for accumulating. In the darkness of her late night research sessions, Asori sometimes mused that the eyes of her assemblage watched over her, though she was never sure if their intent was protection or destruction.

A satisfied smile spread over the professor's lips as she approached the table in the center of the room. Sitting on its surface was a mask, distinct from its brethren on the wall. This one wrapped completely around the wearer's head. She lifted it gingerly from its holder and held it before her, looking into its eyes. The black feathers were silky smooth under her fingers, the eye cutouts watching her with a blank stare and the yellow bird's beak hung open as if crying out to the heart of the galaxy itself. Inverting it, she looked inside, running her fingers along the edges of the soft lining. She wondered what it felt like wear, to have the whole of it wrapped around her head.

A voice whispered in her mind urging her to put it on, inviting her to look through those eyes. Her mind drifted, straining to hear the secrets the voice kept from her. *'Put on the mask, it will tell you what you want to know,'* it taunted.

"Father?" she whispered. "Where are you?"

Bringing the opening closer to her face she caught a whiff of musty decay. Before she was lost completely to the trance and donned the mask, the scent brought her mind back into sharp focus and she shook her head free of the inviting whispers. Her fingers fumbling as they slipped on the slick feathers, Asori found herself short of breath, with a bead of sweat on her brow. Inhaling deeply, she steadied her grip on the mask and placed it back in its place of awe and honor upon the dark wood table.

Still shaking slightly, Asori retrieved her cup of tea and took a few sips as she looked out the window to clear her mind. It was not the first time she had been caught under the spell of the precious object on the table. Since it came into her possession, her dreams had grown ominous and disturbing, her sleep fitful, and many nights she would wake in the dark, the shadows in her room seeming to flutter around her and the whisper of birds wings echoing in her ears.

With a sigh, she took a final sip of tea and placed the cup on the desk. If dark dreams and a haunting presence in her mind were the price she must pay to achieve her goals, then so be it. Glancing at the digital display on her desk, she was surprised to see how time had flown by her and turned her attention back to the preparations for her journey.

Opposite the wall of silent sentinels, the other side of the study was lined from floor to ceiling with shelving. It was loaded to bursting with databooks, notepads and loose, tattered folders, their age and material lending a musty scent to the air in the room despite the advanced air circulation system. Dictionaries of symbology, old maps, and detailed accounts of tribal rituals sat side by side on the shelves along with the doctor's own published works.

Moving to the shelves, Asori began scanning the contents, her hands moving with deft assurance as she selected volumes, humming a child's lullaby to herself as she worked. Arms loaded to capacity, she carried the databooks and other materials to a sleek wooden desk facing the window. She sat and began combining files to a blank databook. Well entrenched in the process within minutes, the chime of her personal comm rang a few times before it garnered her attention.

"Asori Kapradina, here," she spoke with the absent-mindedness of one otherwise occupied as she pressed the 'accept call' button.

A young man's face appeared on the small screen. He was sweating despite the snow swirling around him, all color drained from his face. "It's done, milady. Just like you told me. Everything is gone."

Anger sweeping over her visage, Asori's tone was harsh and lashing. "Why are you calling me here? I told you to never contact me at home unless it was a dire emergency. This little update was not an emergency, was it?"

"N..No, milady, it wasn't," the young man stammered as his good news was greeted by an angry outburst.

Asori sighed before continuing in a calmer tone. She knew from experience there was no point agitating the man any further or he would stop listening to what she had to say. "Well, what's done is done. Wait at the arranged meeting place and Faza will tell you what to do next."

"Yes, milady. My apologies," he groveled, then perked up as a thought entered his mind. "Will... will I be seeing you again before the rendezvous?"

"No, Ceril. You will not." She shook her head, frustration forming a crease in her brow. "Now just wait there for Faza, can you handle that?"

His disappointment evident, he pouted. "Yes, milady. I can wait..."

"Good, see that you do." She clicked off the comm before the man could continue, cursing him even after his image disappeared. "Damnable fool. The things I put up with for you, Grandfather."

Rubbing her eyes with the heels of her hands for a moment, she gave a heavy sigh before returning to her task. The door chime rang at the far side of the apartment and a moment later, Javes came in, announcing a visitor.

A beaming smile spread over Asori's face and she leapt from her seat as a tall, dark haired woman entered the room.

"Faza, darling!" Asori called out to her. "I am so glad you've arrived safely!"

"Milady." The other woman gave Asori a deep bow, a sly grin on her lips.

Asori playfully smacked her friend on the shoulder. "Stop that this instant. We've known each other for far too long for that business."

Pulling the woman up from her supplicant posture, Asori wrapped her in a tight hug before releasing her and stepping back. Dressed in her favored soft green, the slim cut of Faza's pants were hidden beneath a surcoat that clung at the top, flaring at the waist into a loose garment that trailed to her feet. The subtle bulge of a leg holster the only visible clue that the woman was not an academic friend.

"Excited yet?" she asked, standing now at her full height and towering over her friend.

"Of course I'm excited." Asori's eyes grew bright as she spoke. "After all these years, all this work, I may finally get my family back."

"May? If anyone can do it, it's you, Asori," Faza assured her. "I've never seen anyone so single-minded, even in such a worthy cause."

"Yes, it is worthy, isn't it? Can you imagine the possibilities?" A tear came to the doctor's eye, her voice growing deeper with emotion. "No one need ever suffer as I do, the daily memory of losing those nearest and dearest will be a thing of the past."

Grasping Asori by the shoulders, giving her an affectionate squeeze, Faza lead her to the chairs in the center of the room. "It will be a blessing to the whole galaxy and all will know that you are the one who brought it about."

Plopping into the comfortable seat and swinging her legs over the arm, Asori clicked her tongue and chided. "Now you're sounding like one of my little cultists, Faza."

"Well, it is true, you know," the other teased before her tone became more serious. "Just remember who got you there once you're on top of the world, okay?"

Placing a hand on Faza's knee, Asori reassured her friend. "Darling, I could never forget all you've done for me." Hesitating a moment, she considered her next words carefully. "Speaking of doing things for me, I need you to tie up a very large loose end before we leave Acking."

"Sure, Boss," Faza teased her with the childhood nickname. "What do you need?"

Rubbing her hand along her forehead to release the tension there, Asori explained. "Ceril put the entire effort at risk yesterday and, while he cleaned up the mess, I fear he is not trustworthy enough to carry out any other tasks. He seems to have made himself very expendable and yet I cannot simply cut him loose. He knows too much."

With a wave of her hand, Faza cut her off before she could continue. "Say no more, my dear. It will be dealt with before you reach your ship."

"Thank you, Faza. You are a true friend." A tired smile passed over Asori's face. Now it was Faza's turn to place a gentle hand on her friend's knee. Her tone was soft and deadly serious when she spoke. "I've told you since we were kids, Asori, if you ever need me, I'm here for you."

Asori met her eyes and took in the depth of emotion that lay there. Laughing, she covered her friend's hand with her own. "Yes, but who knew when you met that Veasi that you'd be learning the exact skills I would need most urgently?"

Lounging back in the chair, Faza stretched her long, muscled frame. "It's true, things couldn't have worked out better."

"We've much to do before the morning." Asori sighed, rubbing her head again, continuing the fruitless battle against the tension that mounted there.

"Mmmm." Faza agreed, stretching her neck until her head hung over the back of the chair.

"So, any chance I could recruit you to help with some packing?" Asori asked, her voice light once more.

A broad grin flashed across Faza's face as she leapt up before kneeling once again at Asori's feet. Her friend's difficulty focusing on any task outside of academia had been long standing joke between them for years. "Your wish is my command."

Chapter 9
Cometh the revelator

Lower Levels, Torant City, Acking

Wind howled through the deep canyons shaped by the buildings of Torant City. Stirring up the snow, the gusts created the illusion of a raging blizzard, though the storm had ended a few days earlier. Battling against the encroaching darkness, the greenish-yellow glow of low-powered lighting struggled on its own--the sun giving up its futile battle to send its rays to the surface hours before.

The narrow passageways of the lower levels were bordered with homes and businesses crammed in shoulder to shoulder, foundation to foundation, each propping up its neighbor as ever more structures were built on top of them. The scent of rot and decay permeated the air all throughout the district, even the freezing cold of winter did little to quelch the odor.

On one of these cramped, decaying streets the air lightened, making breathing easier. Streetlights did not struggle with the same futile effort as elsewhere and the smell was not so strong. A stoop leading to one of the doorways was kept clean and neat with the exception of a few bowls of food, circled with enthusiasm by a cadre of alley cats.

Within the cozy house, so out of place among its dilapidated neighbors, the walls creaked and groaned with the ceaseless wind, cold air seeping through the cracks in the windowsills, seeking the spots of warmth that eluded their icy grasp, dancing in an endless chase as the air currents shifted, fluttering the curtains in their wake.

Opening her eyes, Grannie Hella felt a lingering sense of discomfort sitting like a weight upon her chest. She sat up, the thick comforter falling back as she swung her legs over the edge of the bed. A shiver ran down her back as the collected heat of an evening's slumber leeched from the bedclothes. Standing up with a hearty yawn, the grey-haired woman grumbled under her breath. The sheets would take far too long to warm back up when she returned.

Pulling on her robe and woolen slippers to ward off the icy chill from the floor, she lit the hand-held lantern sitting on her nightstand and headed for the stairs leading down to her common room. A moment later the light went out and, with a muttered curse, she smacked the bottom of the unit until it sputtered back to life.

"Damn Rendolan leftovers," she complained to the night air that seemed to laugh as it swiped more heat from her shivering frame. "Wait, it's na their time yet. Got's ta shake off this sleep."

Shaking her head, she stood there pondering for a moment before waving a hand in the air, a wide grin spread across her wrinkled face as she cried out. "Ah! That's it! Damn Diot leftovers!"

"Now," she continued her conversation with the dark

nothingness that surrounded her. "Why am I awake at this unholy hour?"

She paused at the base of the stairs, listening to something unseen "Ah, yes, yes, of course. They'll be arriving any minute now, won't they?"

With a nod of satisfaction, Grannie moved through the common room and into the kitchen. The cramped space was jammed with utensils, pots, pans and crockery. She moved about the tightly-packed room with practiced ease, paying little mind to the task at hand as she hummed to herself. A few moments later she placed a tray loaded with a porcelain teapot, two cups, a plate of sandwiches, and a decadent pile of cookies on the low table of her common room. With the light scent of meat wafting through the air and water sloshing over her hand, she placed two bowls side by side upon the floor nearby.

Glancing up at the clock, Grannie nodded, pulling an extra wrap around her shoulders as she walked to the front door. One more quick glance at the little clock on the entryway table and she opened the door.

There was a swirl of snow before the air cleared and a man appeared, his long coat wrapped around him as he stood there, a finger poised to press the door chime button. Recovering from his initial surprise with as much dignity as he could muster, he gave a polite nod to the woman in the doorway.

"Grannie Hella?" the man was unsure if he was addressing the correct person, doubt swirled around him like the snow. "I apologize for the late hour, but there is much that may depend on the information I carry and my apprentice and I sense you are the person we need to see about it."

"Yes, yes, I know," she told him, pulling him through the doorway with more strength than would be expected in one so aged. "Now you and yer scolyt get in here before ya catch yer death."

Before he understood exactly what was going on, Elys Ki Dul found himself sitting in a comfortably overstuffed chair, his coat hanging on a hook and a warm cup of tea in his hands. Learza was sniffing all around the room, seeming to be at complete ease with the situation while he himself was a bit flustered.

"Mistress Hella, I..." he began before Grannie cut him off, waving her hand in his face.

"None of that 'Mistress' business. Time gets wasted on formalities like that, young man. Call me Gran," she told him as she plopped with casual informality onto the couch across from him and began pouring her own cup of tea.

"As you wish... Gran." He nodded his head before continuing. "I will not keep you; I see you have other guests coming?"

Shaking her head, Gran smiled as Learza came and put her head in the old woman's lap. "Me? No, not a t'all," she told Elys as she scratched Learza's ears.

His scolyt 's forward nature seemed to please the old woman, though Elys thought he might need to have another chat with her about approaching strangers in such a manner. The lecture would wait, right now there was still a lack of clarity and a sense of unease surrounding his entire situation. Elys realized that the comfort and predictability he had grown accustomed to were left behind from the moment he decided to look for this woman.

He and Learza had spent the entire day roaming the lower levels near the enclave, searching for any clue to Grannie's location. No one they asked had ever heard of her. Evening fell and the wind picked up, chilling them to the bone as they continued their search. They kept looking, neither even suggesting that they turn back until at last Learza caught a glimmer of someone's Blessing, bright and out of place in the cold damp of their surroundings. She tracked it alone until Elys, too, began to sense it and, picking up their pace, they had arrived at the little house jammed in amongst a sea of structures in the bowels of the city. The fraer had barely caught his breath when the door flew open and the odd little woman yanked him into her house a few minutes before, leaving him in his current swirl of confusion.

"But you have tea all ready for visitors?" he questioned, indicating the tray piled with an array of food intended for special company as he tried to make sense of why she would be receiving visitors at this late hour.

Gran gave him a wink and patted his knee. "Waiting for you, dear. And your sweet scolyt, too." Scrubbing Learza's face between her hands, Gran laughed when the dog looked up at the woman, meeting her eyes before stepping back from her as if bitten.

'Sa, she's glowing!' The stunned reaction spasmed through their bond, heavy with static.

Sensing Learza's distress, Elys reached out, scanning the room. He sensed his scolyt near him, but froze when he reached Gran. Her presence was like a nebula, a million suns being born and destroyed within the space of her petite frame. It wasn't that she was Blessed, it was more that she was of the Void itself. The light flared, then went out and he found his attention thrust back into the moment.

"Careful there, me boy. You'll be hurtin' y'self." Gran's voice was quiet and consoling as she grasped his hand.

"Beg pardon?" he looked up at her, shaking his head to clear the dazed thoughts, and he caught a glint of starfire in her eyes.

Gran lifted his chin to meet her eyes once more. "Some of us, we canna go too naked in the world, can we? Burn out other's eyes, we would."

Elys sat there, unable to react as the impact of Gran's identity sunk into his mind like a stone.

'Sa, she's beautiful, isn't she?' Learza, processing her initial shock with surprising ease, curled up next to Gran's feet.

Elys nodded his head slowly, understanding reaching his mind at last as a smile spread over his lips. *'Yes, scolyt, she is.'*

Elys came to kneel before Gran, a gesture of respect and deference in the presence of a great being and one not lightly given by one of the Hantirri order.

"You... your kind... are supposed to be legend, myth." His voice was filled with awe.

"What's supposed to be an' what is ain't always the same thing." She yanked on his tunic, pulling him from his bow. "Now up ya get. I'll have none of that bowin' and scrapin'. I'm a living, breathing being, t'same as you."

The spell Elys found himself under faded back as he took his seat once more. The realization that these dingy, cramped surroundings conflicted with the power and beauty of the being before him prompted him to question her. "Why do you hide yourself here? You should be in a place of honor."

"And be poked and prodded? My every word recorded as folk look fer clues to the future an' answers to the past?" she scoffed, shaking her head with firm defiance. "No, thank you kindly. I deserves me privacy, just like anyone else. Which brings us 'round to the reason yer here, doesn't it? What information do ya have what's so all important that ya need to drag these sorry, old bones int' it?"

Confusion once again clouding Elys's mind, he sought to confirm that he understood her question. "Forgive me, Gran, but you knew when we were coming, to the very second, yet you do not know why we are here?"

"I never said I was omnipotent, boy." She grinned at him, poking him in the ribs.

"Yes, ma'am." He nodded, grinning as he began to relax. He liked her, he couldn't help himself. The air around her vibrated with light and there was no doubt in his mind that no matter what followed, he was right in seeking this being out.

His tone grew more serious as he began his explanation at last. "We, Learza and I, came in contact with the Tirtet enclave on Heronat. They passed us a message regarding the resurrection of the Ilandu and indicated we should contact you specifically."

Gran's jovial expression faded into one of concern. She tapped her lips with her finger, pondering the information. "The diary's been stolen then, has it?"

Elys crinkled his face, his bewilderment breaking through the mask of calm he struggled to maintain. "Why, yes. But..."

"I also dinna say I didn't know anything a t'all, young one," she told him, pointing a finger at him in admonishment.

She then sat back further in her chair, giving him an appraising look that seemed to search his soul. With any other being, Elys would say it was colloquialism, but with Grannie, he knew that she truly was looking into the depths of his being. The thought gave him both a wild sense of wonder and an awestruck chill at what she might find.

Finding the information she sought, though Elys was at a loss as to what it could be, Gran gave a firm nod of her head and waved at him with a hurrying gesture. "Now ya just drink up that tea and we'll be gettin' down ta business."

Chapter 10
Just below the surface

Lower Levels, Torant City, Acking

Empty cups held the last dredges of tea, the grit of the remaining leaves undrinkable and left to grow cold. Grannie Hella lifted the cup farthest from her and peered into it, careful not to jar the contents at the bottom. Turning the chipped porcelain counterclockwise, she paused for a moment, then grinned as she spotted a few shapes to her liking formed in the leaves.

"So how deep does your little rabbit hole run, my boy?" she asked Elys, placing the cup back on the tray with a satisfying clink.

Wiping a few crumbs from his mouth as he placed an empty plate on the table, Elys cocked his head and looked her in the eye. "I'm afraid I don't understand."

"How indoctrinated 'ave they got ya? Do ya know of the prophecy of the Cloven Swords?" Watching his reaction out of the corner of her eye, she began piling napkins and empty plates onto the tray. Elys inched forward on his seat, beginning to help her without being asked.

"Yes, all Hantirri know it. We are taught of its importance as initiates," he answered, curious as to where the prophecy would fit into all of this. "Done, Learza?" he asked the scolyt at his feet as he reached down to retrieve her bowls.

'Yes, Sa,' she replied, licking the edges of her mouth with her pink tongue. *'That was really good!'*

"Hmm, aye." Gran nodded as she worked. "Can see why they'd do that, thinkin' they got it all figured out. Ignorant fools dunno what they're in fer."

Elys froze, an empty bowl in his hands, "In for? Is the order in danger? Is the federation under threat?"

Gran waved him off, continuing to clean the crumbs from the table in her calm, efficient manner. "Oh, tha's just me ramblin' agin, don't worry y'self."

Dropping the bowl on the table with a bit more force than he intended, Elys let a trace of frustration through in his tone. "You hint that the Hantirri order is in danger of destruction, and possibly the Diot along with it, and then tell me not to worry? I've sat here for half the night, and while I appreciate the tea and food, I still do not know why I am here. Gran, what is in that diary?"

Gran sighed and sat back into her seat, leaving the dirty dishes to sit. "There's no need to get testy, young one. There's much to tell and it's best not received on an empty stomach is all."

Learza put her head on Gran's lap and when the old woman patted the sofa next to her, the dog jumped up and curled her tail around herself as she settled into the cushion.

'Scol? Is that proper behavior?' Elys, regretting that his tone was tinged by his frustration with Grannie Hella,

followed the comment with a quick little wave of warmth through their bond.

'I asked her and she said it was okay, Sa.' Learza explained as if her reasoning should be obvious. *'She said there was going to be a long story and I might as well be comfortable.'*

Finding it odd that he had been unaware of their conversation, Elys's thoughts were thrown a bit off track. The bond with his scolyt showed nary a ripple during her communication with Gran and the thought bothered him. 'Alright, young one. Next time try not to be so forward and wait for the invitation.'

'Yes, Sa.' Learza replied with a whisper.

When Elys returned his attention to Gran, he found she was watching him closely. None had ever before been able to access the bond he shared with Learza, yet he had the distinct sense that the old woman had listened to every word they said and was waiting for them to finish before she began speaking again. Remembering the power that lay dormant in the being before him, Elys relaxed his guard, releasing his frustration and preparing to listen to her story with an open mind.

With a nod of acknowledgment from the young Hantirri, Gran began her tale. "Where to begin now? Yes, we'll start with the diary's owner, shall we? Aedan Kapradina was a sore powerful man. His family dinna give him over to the Hantirri when they came 'round knocking. They distrusted the Hantirri, and with good reason at the time, mind you. Aedan grew up and 'is Blessing flourished. He was taught by a trusted family advisor, an Ilandu who heard o' the young man's talents. He was taught the ways of the Ilandu and started callin' 'isself Naraka, 'dark strength'. And he was a bad un, let me tell ya."

Elys felt power rippling around them in strange patterns, almost as if spectral beings were circling them, listening to their conversation. "He was one of the last Ilandu to be destroyed at the end of the wars, wasn't he? Surely there is nothing left of him except that book; all his followers were killed on Vestra. Who would even know that diary existed?"

"That, my boy, is part of the puzzle I'm tryin' to figure out." Gran tapped a finger against her lips as she thought. "It's not his followers that concern me, no. Only one o' his bloodline could raise him up and the last a his descendents were killed many a year ago."

Quiet fell between them for a moment. A feeling of icy fingers running along his back traced a shiver down Elys's spine. He felt a nudge and his eyes dropped to the pile of dirty dishes on the table before being drawn to a blinking, old newsreader sitting nearby. Scanning the daily feed of reports absentmindedly gave his thoughts a chance to coalesce and his mind began to digest this new flood of information. A name crossed the screen, catching his eye and his stomach lurched. Grabbing the scuffed, ancient reader, he brought up the full story. Sensing her mentor's distress, Learza's head perked up and she gave him a gentle nudge through their bond. Barely taking a second to acknowledge her, Elys looked up at Gran, the color fading from his face.

"Gran," his voice was soft, unsure. "the name of Kapradina still lives on."

"No, no, young one, they're all gone now." She waved her hand at him, dismissing the comment as she poured herself another cup of tea.

"No, they're not." Holding up the reader so she could see it, he watched as her eyes went wide with shock. A short article on Dr. Asori Kapradina, sole survivor of the Kapradina line and rising star of the academic world, glowed a dull green on the aging screen.

Saying nothing, Gran closed her eyes and Elys felt the air shift around him as she probed the Void for threads of possibility.

"So, it is true," Elys said, his voice catching in his throat. "The Ilandu found a way to return from the Void. In her hands, that book could destroy us all."

"Not necessarily." Gran opened her eyes, a tinge of grey clouding the bright sheen of their surface. "The diary's got a ritual wot would raise the dead, tha's so. Now, it's not just as simple as reading the words, mind you. There's a mask involved, a bird's head. T'was lost in the Shambles many years ago, I dunno where it went to. And there must be a sacrifice as well. Somethin' must be given up to gain that kind of power, no lie."

Elys continued reading the short article, searching for any clues that could aid them in finding this woman. Battling the fears swirling through his mind, he came across the information he hoped he would not find. Speaking with a voice void of emotion, he told her, "Gran, it says here she's an expert on symbology and famed for her collection of rare masks."

"Oh dear." Gran shook her head and sighed, her shoulders

slumping as if under a great weight. "Well. Things 'ave started shiftin' quicker then. Now why did I na see her, right under me nose? Too caught up in th'day to day, me thinks. Lost sight a the bigger picture, me."

Pondering what their next step should be, most likely to notify the Synod, Elys took a deep breath and thrust his fears to the side. The return of the Ilandu was especially dangerous to the order at this time, swinging as it was in its precarious state of unease within the federation community. Still, one Ilandu disciple could be easily defeated by the strength of the Hantirri and, on his own, how much trouble could he truly cause? A further question plagued Elys' mind, one that part of him knew would put all the pieces together, explaining the bad feeling growing in his stomach.

"But what does that have to do with the prophecy of the Cloven Swords?" he asked, preparing himself for Gran's answer.

She shifted uncomfortably in her seat for a moment, avoiding eye contact as Elys watched her every move. She smiled, impressed by the determination present in his steady stare. She sensed the self doubt wash away from his mind when the fraer pulled on reserves he kept deeply banked down. Realizing that while she might force him to accept a more simple answer, it would not serve him in the days to come. She prepared to answer his questions.

She sighed, prefacing her story with a warning. "What I tell ya now, you gots to take on faith. It's not all typed up and neat in the Books of Blessed and Cursed and you've just gotta take me word on it."

Elys looked into her eyes once more. Reflecting on all she already told him, he remembered the fire he glimpsed within her, the depth of power he could barely fathom. Faith would be easy to come by when the words came from this being. "I understand, Gran."

"Alrighty then." Giving him a firm nod, she continued. "Naraka, the Ilandu what developed tha' ritual? He knew the prophecy well. It were his obsession, ta say the least 'bout it. It were his personal mission ta obliterate it from existence, along with any folk who might fulfill it. Nothin' would stop 'im, not even death. We thought he were done, 'is body buried along with the rest a his army instead of burnt proper. Rumours flew after the war, some true, some lies. When word got 'round tha Naraka's remains were secreted away somewheres, we feared the worst. It'd take time, but we knew there were a chance 'e might return. The search began for 'is body, but more importantly, we 'ad to protect the prophecy. It comes from Tir itself, ya see. We're not always meant to know why Tir directs us to do its Will, we just 'ave to do what it wants us to, don't we? And so fer safety, we sent the scion underground."

"Scion?" Elys had never heard of any particular person, nor their descendants, related to the prophecy. Pits of doubt in the surface of his beliefs spread like cracks through ice on a winter's day. The path of Tir's Will grew more treacherous in his mind.

Gran grinned at his stunned reaction. There would be more shocks to come for this young man in the days ahead if she was seeing things properly. Tir was leading him now and there was no turning back. "Yes, my boy. Now if ya keep repeating what I'm sayin' we'll get nowhere, will we?"

"No, ma'am." Elys shook his head. Glancing over at Learza, he reached out to her through their bond. She was perfectly at ease, absorbing all Gran told them and taking it in stride. His scolyt's easy going nature and connection to the ever-changing Void aided her greatly when things got rough. He, on the other hand, was beginning to develop a knot of tension at the base of his skull, a familiar reminder that he often thought too hard about things instead of letting them flow.

He returned his attention to Gran as she continued her explanation, her voice lilting through the information with the ease of old knowledge. "Now then, the prophecy's built on a particular lineage, one what's got power in its blood, one chosen by Tir special ta produce the Wielder of the Unified Sword. The scion was sent to a distant planet, removed from those she was livin' with and hidden along with her guardians."

Elys found his thoughts focusing on the most hidden and unobtrusive order of ascetics he could think of. "The Tirtet?" he asked, the recent encounter with that order bringing them easily to mind.

Gran nodded, impressed by his deduction, there was hope for this one yet. "Yes, young one. They might seem insular and uninterested, but they're deep involved in upholdin' the prophecy."

"So, where is their enclave, where is the scion?" Chewing over the problem in his mind, Elys wondered how the Synod would plan to protect this scion and the prophecy.

"The guardians protectin' the scion live in a hidden

enclave, not one tha's known to anyone. T'was decided that to protect the scion's identity, she be hidden, her secret known only to a very few." Gran explained, watching Elys' reaction and recognizing the furrow in his brow as a sign of his forethought.

"The scion is a normal human?" he asked, a bit surprised that Tir would chose a simple human to carry out its Will, rather than some long-lived being of great wisdom like Gran. Elys wondered what this person was like and how they handled the burden of their destiny. He knew it would be more than he could handle himself.

"Yes, the scion's a girl, always is. The current one's 'bout your age if I'm not mistaken. It's from her offspring the Wielder'll appear, but that's for the future so you've no need to worry 'bout none of that." Reaching over the table, Gran patted Elys' knee and gave him a quick wink. "Now, she don't know all the details of her destiny, ya know. She dunna know that she's the mother of the Wielder. And she don't know much about the Hantirri, neither. She's led a quiet life 'til now."

'Is she Blessed, Gran?' Learza, silent until that moment, hopped off the couch and went to her mentor's side. Absently, he rubbed her head, just behind the ears and she felt him relax a little with the action.

Shaking her head, Gran answered the scolyt. "That, I dunna know, I've not seen 'er since she was a wee one. Some o' her ancestors 'ave been sensitive ta Tir's Will, but I dunna know if this scion has it in her."

Learza, having heard enough information to move forward, was ready for action. *'What do we do next, Gran?'*

The old woman smiled at the canine, giving her an approving nod for her readiness. "Well, I have a task of me own to do. If the child of Naraka's blood is tryin' to raise her ancestor, there are tools that need acquirin'.

You and your Sa here'll be goin' to retrieve the scion. She must be protected on tha journey."

"But wouldn't she be safer where she's hidden?" Elys questioned her.

"Things be shiftin' fast now. The scion 'as a destiny. It be time for her ta come out of hidin' and fulfill her part of the prophecy," Gran answered as she returned her attention to the dirty dishes on the table.

Elys shook his head. "That's all well and good, Gran, but I cannot go. This is not a task for me, nor Learza. I am not powerful, I'm no hero. This should be brought to the synod, let someone like Anos Keener take the mission. He's sure to bring it success."

Gran's eyes lit with a hint of the fire she held banked down within her. Her voice lost it's strange lilt and took on a clear tone of authority. "This is more than a mission, young one. There are larger things at stake here than the survival of the Hantirri or the Diot. It may not seem it, but the galaxy is at a fragile place in its history, more fragile than I've seen it in many, many years. There is no debate on this. Tir chooses the messenger and those it wants for its tasks. You are here and the time is now, Elys Ki Dul."

Chapter 11
Laying the course

Lower Levels, Torant City, Acking

"I cannot be the one, Gran. This is a task for a hero, not a Hantirri who barely qualifies as a courier." Elys shook his head once more, the crease that appeared in his brow furrowing more deeply. "I'm not powerful enough for this."

Gran crossed her arms over her chest, bewildered frustration on her face. "So even though Tir's Will led ya to me, even though ya be the only one to see the signs fer what they are, you're gonna pass this task off 'ta another?"

"Yes, ma'am," Elys replied with a sigh and a subtle slump of his shoulders. Something tickled at his thoughts, urging him to listen to its whispers, but he pushed it aside, determined that he was not the one to fulfill the mission.

Gran cocked an eyebrow at him. "And do ya think yer high-an-mighty' Synod'll believe ya when ya tell 'em their precious prophecy is in danger?"

Turning the idea over in his mind, Elys considered what he knew of the prophecy. The Wielder was to merge the two cloven swords of Tir, the Sword of Light and the Sword of Dark into the Unified Sword of All. However, no one ever seemed to explain what that truly meant, nor what would happen afterwards. With one sword somewhere here in the Universe, the All that Is and the other in the Void, the All that Was and Shall Be, the task always seemed impossible, mythic. Now the knowledge of a scion, a lineage that would bring the Wielder into the world, changed all that. The possibility of someone returning from death, from the Void, opened up another possibility. Had the Ilandu found a way to bring the Sword of Light here from the Void? When the Wielder appeared and completed the task, would Tir retreat and leave the galaxy without its spirit center? Ideas swirled in the Hantirri's mind as he tried to make sense of the obtuse phrasing of the words he memorized in his youth.

And the Synod, what would they say when he brought news of Gran's existence? They had already rendered their decision, but would physical proof sway their minds? Would they continue to do all in their power to protect the order and the Diot, even to the point of jeopardizing the ancient prophecy?

"I do not know," he admitted, thoughts churning through his mind in dizzying patterns, clouding his ability to sort the problem out.

"This ain't just about the bloody Hantirri and their high holy crusade ta rescue the galaxy from i'self." Gran's voice took on a deep passion and fire. "The prophecy'll bring about Tir's Will, not the Hantirri's. It's chosen you for this trial." She pointed a finger in Elys' direction, emphasizing her words. "That should be enough for ya."

Learza scrunched herself deeper into the couch and Elys appeared as if he had just been slapped. Realizing her lapse of control unleashed a burst of power that startled her companions, Gran's face softened, her frustration sliding aside as she prompted Elys to try a different approach to his confusion. "Listen ta Tir's Will, Elys, tha's what the Hantirri are Blessed ta do, ain't it? The Synod ain't the only ones what can hear the Will. The energy humming through yer own body, it's got a voice of its own and yer quite well equipped to listen to it yerself, make yer own decisions. Ya've trained yer whole life ta hear its message, haven't ya?"

Seeming to not hear her words, Elys regained his courage, plunging along the line of thought that bothered him most. "Are you saying that the order is dispensable, Gran? That we're not meant to continue? Our time is drawing to an end?"

Shaking her head at his unconscious dismissal of her assistance, Gran explained, "That I canna say, lad. All I can tell ya is the prophecy must be protected, regardless of the cost. The Hantirri ain't the only ones that know of it, and tha puts it in grave danger."

Elys closed his eyes. Things were moving quickly and he needed to center himself. Listening to Tir's Will echoing through the Void as Gran suggested, he felt the threads of the future shifting, unraveling and reweaving themselves into a fine, new tapestry of possibility. At his core Elys knew there was more to what Gran was saying, that the coming events would change his life. The end of the Hantirri, though? The thought frightened him for a moment before he let his fear go with a prayer. The Void would return it to him, renewed as courage and strength. The Hantirri rule ordered his life, but it was simply there to give people the methods and structure to follow Tir's Will. It provided a channel for Blessings that could otherwise be dangerous.

The prophecy was passed to the Hantirri by the voice of Tir itself. There would be no turning from the path once he committed himself to aiding that voice and doing its Will with the fullness of his heart. Somewhere deep inside him, a thread of light appeared and he knew things would work out as they should. Major change would barge into his life whether he wished it or not and all would flow more smoothly if he went with the flow rather than fought it.

Gran watched the Hantirri's countenance, the first rays of daylight through the window illuminating his features, highlighting the little scars and worry lines across his face. The furrow in his brow deepened as he took in all she told him, processing it and weighing the truth of her words. Gradually, the creases smoothed and she felt him letting his fears and expectations for the future slide into the Void.

Nodding her head, she thought to herself. *'He's lettin' it all go fer now, but the doubt'll return. He's gonna to be sorely tested afore this nasty business is through.'*

'He's got me, Gran, he'll be okay.' Learza's voice poked into Gran's thoughts and she smiled at the scolyt beside her. Shuffling closer to the old woman, Learza nudged her head under Gran's hand, looking for attention.

Obliging the request, Gran scratched under Learza's jaw and massaged the furry face under her fingers. *'Ya just be makin' sure you're the one thing he don't give up on, young one. You'll be keepin' him goin' when things go mad.'*

'Are they going to be that bad, Gran?' Learza's concern for her

mentor's well being rippled through their communication.

Nodding, Gran affirmed Learza's fears. *'Aye, young one, t'will get worse for him afore it gets better. You'll just stick close to him, won't ya?'*

'Yes, ma'am,' Learza replied, the knowledge of her mission prompting her to draw her Blessing around herself as if it were a suit of armor.

'Tha's a good pup.' Gran gently ran a hand over Learza's head. *'Hmm, I wonder how much of a pup you really be... old soul within... very interestin'.'*

Gran continued to stroke Learza's head, garnering rumbling sounds of pleasure from the dog's throat. When she looked back to Elys, she found he was watching them, a hint of smile on his lips.

"Feelin' better?" Gran asked, true concern in her voice.

There was a subtle new light surrounding the Hantirri, a sense of peace centered in his belly that had not been there when he arrived. "Yes, Grannie Hella, thank you."

"That bein' so, there's much ta do and little time ta do it, ain't there? Time to get you two off on yer way now." Gran's tone turned matter-of-fact.

Elys shook his head, avoiding Learza's probing thoughts as he spoke. "It will just be me, I fear. I cannot ask Learza to come with me."

Preparing for her reaction as he spoke, Elys was ready when the crashing wave of indignation hit him full force through the bond he shared with his student. *'But why, Sa? I'll behave! I'll pay attention!'*

Now was the time Elys knew he must be firm. He was the teacher here, after all, wasn't he? "I will most probably be getting myself into some serious trouble with the Synod, young one. I will not burden you with those consequences."

'I'm your scolyt, Sa, I go where you go.' Learza was stubborn, her mental voice insistent and backed by a powerful presence.

"I do not know what we'll be facing, Scol." Drawing on his inner reserves of strength, Elys did his best to steel himself against Learza's pleading. He did not know what this journey may entail and the risk of losing his dear scolyt in the process struck fear into his heart. "I do not want to put you in danger, not yet, you are not ready."

Their bond danced with their inner struggle, Learza pleading, Elys pushing back. Opening up more of the bond between them, Elys caught glimpses of the true power and strength that lay within his student. Probing, he was surprised to find Learza utterly ready to surrender to her fate, as long as they were together.

'I'm not afraid, Sa. I'm coming with you. I have to.'

Elys sighed, rubbing his forehead. Once she made up her mind about something, Learza's determination rivaled that of any human he had ever met. Realizing the damage that could occur in their bond if he were to leave her at the enclave, he reached out, searching the Void and praying for guidance. He felt power swell within him, reassuring him that his path and Learza's lay entwined and, as long as he kept checking for guidance, he would not stray from his course.

Still, as Learza's mentor he was unsure that, despite her assurances otherwise, his charge was quite ready for this kind of mission. "There will be much training for you on the way to our destination and I want you to stick close to my side, young one. Do you understand?"

'Yes, Sa! When do we leave?' Learza jumped off the couch, running over to him. Putting her paws up on his shoulders, she began licking him, relishing the stunned expression on his dampened face.

"As soon as possible would be best," Gran urged, a huge grin spreading across her mouth as she observed the deep connection between her visitors. "It's no short journey from here."

"We'll leave this morning," Elys replied, laughing and attempting to nudge his scolyt aside with little success.

"You just have to tell us where to go, Gran."

"Didn't mention it yet, did I? Silly me," Gran laughed to herself. Her mind would need to be a bit sharper than usual in the days to come. "Lan, just inside the Shambles."

"Yes, that is about the middle of nowhere. Good choice, Gran." Elys nodded, still smiling as he pushed Learza down and stood from his chair.

Gran rose as well, walking over to a side table and pulling a concealed compartment open. She slipped a locket and its chain out of the drawer and turned to Elys. "This'll help ya with the Tirtet. They won't be 'spectin' ya an' you'll be needin' proof tha' yer not a danger to 'em."

Elys nodded his understanding, accepting the necklace and slipping it into a pocket. Gran gave a curt nod as he headed towards the door. She held his coat out for him, helping him into the garment before turning him to face her.

"Once ya've got her, ya must bring her to me. If all goes

well, we'll be able ta protect her and capture the Kapradina heir afore everything hits the fan."

'Where do we meet?' Learza asked, having regained her composure, though Elys could feel her joy bubbling through their bond.

"Vestra, young one. Vestra," she replied, bending down to hug the dog and slipping a small parcel into her pack.

"May Tir grant you Blessings, Gran," Elys said, signaling Learza to come to his side with a subtle hand gesture.

"And you as well, young Elys," Gran replied, wrapping him in a warm embrace before opening the door.

A cold wind blew into the house, sucking the heat from the entryway as Elys and Learza took their leave. Gran watched them hurry up the street as the first true rays of sunlight made their way down to the shadowy lower levels. A moment later they were out of sight and Gran shut the door against the chill.

"Well, tha' went much better than I remember it," she said, quite pleased with herself. "Now, where did I leave that map?"

Chapter 12
Ancestral ties bind deepest

Klen Castle, Vestra, The Shambles

Snow swirled around the compact ship as legs extended beneath its belly. The pilot set the craft down with expert care onto the snow-covered landing pad then engaged the ramp, the airlock hissing open, allowing in a flurry of snow and icy air. Inhaling then exhaling a deep breath, Asori Kapradina looked over at her traveling companion. Faza seemed the perfect mirror of calm to Asori's open discomfiture, though a lifetime of friendship meant she could see the quiet excitement burning in the warrior's eyes. Asori admired her friend's stoic mask, garnered from years of training. For herself, she could no more hide her excitement than she could grow taller. The years of haunting pain were soon to be at an end and she was savoring every minute of the journey.

Their boots crunched over the snow coating the stone walkway. Night had fallen hours before and the snowstorm blocked the moons from shining down, the inky blackness broken only by the soft light of the sputtering lamps along the path. Ahead of them, the silhouette of an immense, towered, stone structure, aged and worn, interrupted the pattern of the wind, breaking its flow along the immobile rocks of the outer wall.

Passing through the gate, Asori's breath hitched in her throat. Her ancestor's castle stood before her, dim lights shining from upper windows and blazing torchieres burning at the entrance. It took all of her self control not to break into a run, her excitement making her heart pound almost to bursting. Reining herself in as best she could, Asori approached the towering door and began looking for a way to get someone's attention when it opened from the inside. She was expected.

The crowd inside followed her with their eyes, parting for her as she passed through their midst. Dropping back her thick hood, Asori shivered in the lingering chill that clung to her, its icy fingers still leeching through the cracks between the masonry and the heavy iron door as it was closed behind her. The faces of her loyal followers showed open, hungry anticipation, their eyes focused on the box that Faza carried before her.

A middle-aged man approached them, his eyes bright with excitement as he gave them a little bow. "Everything is ready, Asori. His body was just where you said it would be. I must say it was quite ingenious of our predecessors to hide it from the Hantirri."

Asori shivered, her thin frame ill-equipped for the biting chill of winter. Her voice betrayed her anxiousness, taking on a defensive tone when she replied, "My ancestor was powerful. He garnered the respect and loyalty of many. It is little surprise that they would prepare for his eventual return."

"Yes, that is true. It says much about Naraka's power. Our venture should be a success." The man nodded as he walked alongside Asori, guiding her down a dark corridor towards a light at its end.

Her excitement fueling her emotions, the professor stopped to face the man directly. "Should? Of course it will succeed! I have spent my whole life researching this ritual. I assure you, Cabal, it will work."

Putting his hands up before him, the man sought to reassure the volatile academic. "Yes, Dr. Kapradina, I have no doubt about your dedication to this cause."

Giving a sharp nod of her head, Asori turned on her heel and continued down the stone passageway. With a quick exchange of concerned looks, Faza and Cabal followed her through the last door at the end of the corridor. The flickering light of old-fashioned wax candles gave a dim glow to the room, enhancing the rough surface of the stone walls.

Motioning for Faza to place the box on a nearby table, Asori turned to Cabal, her voice still sharp. "Our timing could not be better. The ritual will take place tonight. Now, I will need time to prepare. Leave us."

With a nod and a final, quick glance at Faza, he assented to her request. "As you wish. I will inform the others to ready themselves."

When the door shut behind him, Asori took a deep breath and looked around the room, checking that all was truly ready for the ritual. A low stage had been erected in the spacious room. The ceiling towered above them, its height lost in the shadows where candle flame could not penetrate. One wooden table sat at the edge of the room, holding the black box Faza placed there. In the very center of the stage, a morgue table sat waiting, a bulky form laying on its surface, covered by a pristine white cloth.

Approaching the still form, Asori reached out her hand, placing it gingerly on the sheet. Her flushed excitement shifting to a quiet melancholy, she sighed softly. The body was cold under her fingers, but she did not flinch from its chill as she did from the snow and ice outside. When she spoke, her voice was filled with sorrow and loss. "This is it, Faza. All my work, all my life, and this is it. I almost can't believe I'm going to see my family again. It's been so hard."

"I know, but with your ancestor's help here, you'll have them back soon," Faza reassured her friend, stepping forward and squeezing Asori's shoulder.

Pulling her attention away from the table, Asori turned to face the taller woman. "If you had not been there to help me, Faza dear, I never would have dreamed that it would be possible to raise him. It's just amazing. We'll bring Naraka back to life and then he will help me return my family from the Void. Then we'll all be together and we'll be able to help so many others who have lost loved ones."

Faza gave her one firm nod, the look in her eyes growing colder as she spoke. "I know, my dear, but you must focus now. You cannot dwell on the happy times ahead. You must focus on your family's murderers, on those that tortured and killed your parents, your brother."

Asori nodded. "Yes, you are right. I must be angry, it will feed the ritual."

Letting her mind float back through time, Asori braced

herself for the onslaught of pain her memories would generate. The events of daily life required her to bury these thoughts, keeping them at bay in a vain attempt at maintaining a sense of normalcy. It took little effort to bring the dark thoughts back into focus, for they were often on her mind.

Masks... they had all worn masks. They were nothing like the complex, ornate bird's mask waiting in its box nearby, no, these were little more than simple bags of fabric, meant to hide features and serving little other purpose. There were no faces for Asori to remember, instead it was their tools and devices that painted a swath of misery across her mind. Cold steel, unrelenting in its hardness and honed to numerous fine points flashed before her inner eye. The men that wielded them searched for something, she did not know what. Her father had placed her in a secret passageway and told her to stay there until Javes came to get her.

When the men came she remained hidden, too terrified to move. Only a young girl at the time, she was forced to watch each of her family in turn as they were tortured and killed before her eyes. It was not until years later that she uncovered the truth: those men were searching for the very diary that had led her here tonight. Returning her family from the death that those men caused would be her revenge. Together, she and her family would hunt those men down and let them see what such evil acts can yield.

Seething, Asori opened her eyes, her rage bringing a sour bile up into her throat. "Light the red candles, Faza, and help me with my robe."

Without a word, Faza responded to her friend's order,

watching the woman out of the corner of her eye as she ignited the candles. Asori had to build herself into a frenzied trance, yet still remain in enough control over herself to perform the ritual. So far, she seemed to be well on her way.

Once the blood-red cloak was around her shoulders, it was with a hollow voice that Asori gave her next instruction. "Let the others in."

Nodding, Faza walked to the door and opened it. A stream of people moved into the room, taking their places in rows in front of the stage. They waited in silence, eyes focused on the shrouded body in the middle of the stage. Electricity originating from the crowd increased the tension in the air until it was as taut as a crossbow, ready to spring. The power surging through the group served to deepen Asori's trance, heightening her senses and bolstering the angry rage that threatened to engulf her.

"Friends, now is the time." she cried out, raising her arms as she spoke. "Rile yourselves! Your anger shall feed Naraka and he shall rise!"

As one, the crowd brought forth their most violent, most angry memories. Anger and hatred flowed all around them, lighting their eyes with a carnal depth of hunger. They began swaying on their feet, some emitting low, predatory growls from deep in their throats. Faza closed her eyes, soaking in the palpable energy of the crowd. Her ears were trained on Asori who was quietly chanting under her breath, the words were of an ancient tongue and foreign to her ears. As the energy of the crowd threatened to peak, the chanting grew louder.

"Tir ve tat, vo Tir ve len
Tir arvano rista yera par sen
Gand vo Hant sisa ver benka
*Hanton veh illar menka"**

Asori repeated the words, over and over in an endless chase of phrase. Her voice growing louder and stronger with each cycle, the room began to fade at the edges of her vision. When Faza moved to the box and removed the bird mask, Asori was only vaguely aware of the action. The tall warrior knelt before her friend, placing the soft feathered mask in her hands. There was little left of the woman who, only a few days ago, was worrying over packing her trunks. She had given over completely to the trance. If someone were to stop the ritual now, she would most assuredly be lost to madness.

The feathers were soft under Asori's fingers, their sleek surface the only connection she still had to the world around her. Lifting it over her head, a new voice joined her chanting. Harsh and gravely, she knew this voice, for it had whispered to her often back on Acking. There would be no more taunting, no more waiting. Slipping the inky blackness of the mask over her head, Asori's voice skipped a beat, her breath catching in her throat as the mask gave a short cackle. Taking up the chant once more, Asori's voice was multiplied, a thousand voices intoning the phrases of power as one.

Louder and louder, the many voices streaming from the mask whipped the crowd towards a frenzy. All were swaying on their feet as they began to hum in unison. Faza's face was lit in an otherworldly grimace, a mask of anger and pain. As the chanting reached a peak, the candles blew out, replaced by a disembodied red glow. Shrieking ever louder, the masked form on the stage took the peak of power even higher, threatening to pierce the eardrums of the faithful in the audience.

At this crescendo, the masked form raised its hands over its head and seemed to lift off the ground as it gave a final scream, its voice breaking as the red light went out, plunging the room into utter darkness.

Silence enveloped the space and, for a moment, no one moved, all holding their collective breath. A flash of light blinded the assembled as Faza lit a candle. Asori, still masked and swaying in time to an unheard music, stood at her ancestor's feet. A subtle shift of movement brought everyone's attention to the sheet on the table.

Pushing the shroud aside, for the first time in over a century, Lord Naraka, leader of the Ilandu, sat up and looked around the room.

Deep scars were etched on his face and hastily repaired injuries remained stitched in field dressing like a map across his features. There was no glow of life in his eyes. The deathly pallor to his skin, pulled taut across his bones, made him a terrifying visage in the dim light of a single candle. After a moment's hesitation, he leapt to his feet, crouching low to the ground as he landed. Growling and grunting, he scanned the crowd back and forth, his dull eyes searching for something. Freezing when his scrutiny reached Asori, he dove toward her. She made no move to stop him, still lost in the trance and pliable to his rough hands.

Knocking his heir to the ground, Naraka moved too quickly for anyone to save her, had they been brave enough to approach the newly raised man. Some would later take solace in the idea that Asori was too far into the trance to feel the breaking of her own spine or the snapping of the ligaments and tendons that kept her head attached to her neck. A sickening crack echoed through the room as Dr. Kapradina's skull smashed against the stone floor, sending the bird mask flying off in the opposite direction. Yowling with bloodthirsty excitement, Naraka crawled to the oozing head, reaching down to grab at the grey matter leaking from the open wound and slurping down the contents.

The crowd watched in nauseated wonder as Naraka's eyes cleared, a bright intelligence settling in where before only a vacant stare resided before. A subtle shift overtook his skin, it softened at the edges, a bit of color rising in cheeks that until then were only a deathly green.

Holding her breath, Faza approached him, her movements smooth and subtle. Kneeling before him, she bowed her head, the room growing tense once more with her act of submissive trust. "My lord, Naraka."

The Ilandu stood and looked down at her before turning his attention to the rest of the crowd, scanning them for familiar faces and cataloging their number in his mind. Taking a deep breath, he pulled the scattered power of the ritual about himself, leaving the crowd with the distinct impression that with it he took a bit of their own life energy, binding them to him.

"It is good to be back."

Chapter 13
An ember begins to flame

Enroute to Lan, The Shambles

In the days that followed their departure from Acking, Learza worked harder than she ever had before. Impressing her mentor with her maturity and dedication, she honed the gifts of Tir's Blessing until they were as sharp as Elys had ever seen them. She developed strong mental shields to hide her Blessing from others, a skill Elys admittedly envied. Elys also began teaching her to manipulate the light around her. It was said that those Blessed with the strongest gifts could use light as a weapon, but neither Elys nor his scolyt had this particular ability. Learza worked until she was at least able to direct a broad beam of light into a zig-zag pattern down the darkened hold of the ship.

Elys, too, trained for the unknown trials to come. With only one or two minor exceptions, the last few years gave him no cause to use the long knives he carried. Courier work had made him soft, vulnerable and lazy without his realizing it. Learza would watch him with rapt attention as he swung his blades in the tight confines of the Hantirri ship carrying them to Lan. The steel was finely forged, the blades light and quick. Wielding them without injury to oneself or the surrounding space required fine manipulation and a steady hand. Tired muscles, long out of use, gradually regained their memory until the hilts once again felt like old friends in his hands.

Nightly meditations honed their minds as well, strengthening the thread that bound them until Elys wondered if anything could break it. Through his bond with Learza, Elys was allowed a more powerful connection to the Void, the depths of her heart revealing a wider network of possibility than he ever had access to on his own. Together they explored many of the paths Tir offered them, working to understand their own purpose and the subtle changes occurring in their relationship.

Meditating on the shifting bond with his scolyt, Elys was startled when an alarm went off, indicating the beginning of their approach sequence. Moving to the controls, he prepared the craft for landing, the big blue and brown world of Lan growing larger in the viewport. Upon entering the atmosphere, the craft began to shimmy and shake, the sounds of joints creaking and metal scraping together filling the small cabin. The Hantirri maintained a small collection of ships for personal use, but there had been little selection available when he and Learza had left. This craft appeared the most space-worthy of the bunch. Wondering if he had been wrong in choosing it, Elys gingerly piloted the craft to the ground, the landing jets misfiring as the ship came down with jolting impact onto the planet's surface.

Little fanfare greeted the duo as they passed quickly through the dingy spaceport. Few other ships were parked near their own, a couple of freighters and a mass transport that appeared in no hurry to depart. No one, it seemed, came to Lan without good reason. No officials appeared to check them through customs this time; the Shambles was beyond the reach of Diot bureaucracy. As the Ilandu conflict had raged through the galaxy, residents of the more isolated planets moved toward the better defended planets closer to Acking, leaving only the most steadfast, or poor, settlers behind. When the wars ended and the Zemvo began exerting its influence once more, many independent-minded folk moved back out to the abandoned planets. Each scattered settlement had its own laws and rules, for the most part living in peace despite their harsh lives.

Emerging from the dark terminal, Elys was unsure of where to proceed. Following the scattered flow of foot traffic, he and Learza strolled along with the local populace. Before long they found themselves at the beginning of a wide causeway filled with booths. Awnings of red, blue, green and yellow covered the stalls, shading the sellers and their customers from the warm spring sunlight. Shouting the quality of their wares to the crowds, the merchants tried to entice Elys with brightly-colored cloth or sturdy cook pots. Learza's attention was scattered by the numerous butchers and fishmongers calling to her and her mentor, offering the freshest cuts if only they would stop by.

A crowd of children, chasing each other and laughing as they passed, pushed Elys towards a merchant selling fruits and vegetables. She gave him a warm smile in greeting, waving her hands over the copious baskets of ripe fruits and barrels of dark red dried beans.

"See anything you like, Sir? I've got the fairest prices in the market. Not the best, mind you, but the fairest. You'll not get an inferior muja fruit from my stall, that's for sure."

Elys smiled, Learza joining him as she put her paws onto the counter and began sniffing the fruit. "No, thank you for your offer, but we must be on our way."

Giving the little hand signal that let Learza know it was time to go, Elys turned away and began heading further down the street.

"But sir, I may be able to help you!" the woman called after them.

Looking down at Learza, Elys quirked an eyebrow at his scolyt. In such matters he was quickly learning to pay even closer attention to her instincts than he had before.

'She's nice, Sa. And you are hungry.'

Realizing that indeed his stomach was rumbling, Elys ruffled Learza's head before turning back. The woman gave him a smile and a little curtsey as Elys began examining the array of fruit once more.

"You said you might be able to help me. In what way do you think you could be of service?"

Lifting a large basket from behind the stall, the woman proceeded to fill one of her displays with fresh berries, ripe and red. "You're new to Lan. There's a weight on you, I can... well, sense it."

"Indeed," he replied, his voice noncommittal in his response.

The woman paused her work, letting the nearly empty basket dangle at her side and placing her free hand on her hip. "If you're looking for trouble, there's none here will aid you. We're a quiet folk out here. Ever since the plague, folks approach life quite a bit different here than they do in the Diot. Life's precious to us and we got no time for troubles."

"I do not look for trouble, I assure you. I'm just trying to locate someone for a friend, I am but the messenger." With a nod, Elys continued looking over the fruit, keeping the woman's attention.

While on the ship, fraer and scolyt had agreed to keep Learza's Blessing as well as her status as a scolyt a secret until they were with someone they considered trustworthy. They hoped none would suspect scrutiny from such an unexpected source, allowing Learza to probe their situation without anyone's knowledge.

'She's Blessed, Sa, and trained. She's got powerful shields.' The message was short and quick, Learza's senses banking back down as quickly as they rose up.

Picking up a few berries and tossing Learza one, Elys shared his thoughts. *'Hmm. Perhaps she's one of the Tirtet we seek.'*

'I hope so, Sa. I think she knows I'm probing her,' Learza replied before locking down her shields.

'Then we shall move on, Scol.'

Selecting a few pieces of fruit, Elys watched the woman as she bagged them up. Handing her the coins to complete the transaction, their hands touched, the woman jumping a little as Elys leaned in towards her.

"May Tir grant you Blessings," he whispered, taking the bag from the woman's hand before slipping away into the crowd.

Watching the duo with a narrowed stare, the woman waited until they were out of sight before throwing a cover over her fruit and securing the curtained doorway closed. Assured that her stall was shut up tight, the woman scurried off in the opposite direction of the Hantirri, still wandering through the market in the distance.

Later in the afternoon, Learza rubbed up against one of the posts of a stall, scratching her back while Elys admired the fine silver work laid out before an elderly craftsman. Lifting a delicately woven bracelet, small stones embedded in its surface, her mentor smiled.

"Beautiful work," he said, his tone one of sincere admiration for the piece.

"But a bit out of your price range today, eh?" the old gentleman cackled.

Elys laughed and nodded his head. "I am afraid so." Placing the piece with careful reverence back upon its black velvet display board, Elys looked over the other bits and bobs the man crafted.

"I've got somethin' for ya. It's not as pretty as that, but the price is right, I'm sure," the man told him, getting off his stool to begin rummaging in a box under the table.

"I assure you that's not necessary," Elys begged off the offer. What would he need with a bauble no matter the price?

"Oh, but my bones tell me it is," the man argued, his voice lilting in the local accent. "Here, this here's been awaitin' for ya."

Grabbing Elys' hand, the man placed a thin brass bracelet in his palm and closed his hand around it. "That there'll bring ya good luck. And your gonna be needing all the luck you can get."

Elys opened his hand. The bracelet glowed in the shaded daylight of the silversmith's covered stall, a hint of dust coating its surface. Wiping the silt away, he admired the warm glow of the metal.

"It is lovely, but I'm afraid I cannot purchase it today. I do thank you for the offer, though." Elys handed the piece back toward the man, but the elder refused to take it.

"It's worth more in the luck it'll bring the giver and the bearer, young man. You just take it," he replied, shooing Elys' hand away.

His humble nature and training meant he knew better than to argue with a gift, and Elys bowed his head in return. "I thank you, then, for the gift of luck to us both."

Elys and Learza spent the afternoon leisurely wandering through the rest of the market. As they walked, Elys made little effort to hide the power of his Blessing, hoping to attract the attention of the scion's guardians. By the time the sun began to drop towards the horizon he carried a small sack filled with provisions for a few simple meals, but other than the fruit merchant, had not sensed a single person who connected to Tir's Will and the Void as he did.

A quick inquiry with one of the locals yielded directions to a small inn not far from the market. Making their way there, Elys stopped Learza and retrieved a pouch of jerky from her vest. They made a game of the journey as Elys tossed a single piece of the cured meat into the air. Learza would watch the morsel until she got a bead on it and with a single, leaping effort, snapped her jaws around it.

The directions given to them by the merchant made the inn easy to find and soon they were settled in a cozy room, complete with kitchenette. The space was a bit cramped, but reminded Learza much of their quarters at Steeltip Enclave. Sniffing every corner of the room twice over gave her something to do while Elys cooked, having eaten her fill on the way here.

'Many people have stayed here, Sa,' she informed him.

Elys chuckled at her thorough, if obvious, observation, knowing full well that Learza could distinguish between the smells of each individual resident. *'Well, that's no surprise Learza, it is an inn after all.'*

Pausing in one corner near the window, Learza shared her latest discovery. *'There was a sickness long ago. This was a hospital.'*

Nodding as he took a few bites of his dinner, Elys replied, thankful that his mental voice was never garbled by a full mouth. *'That would make sense. I believe the Noravian plague near the end of the wars reached to the very edges of the galaxy.'*

A melancholy seeped through their bond as Learza continued. *'There was sadness, too.'*

'Yes, many died during the sickness, but Lan seems to be overcoming that dark past. The folk here seem truly happy and at peace,' Elys consoled his charge, wishful that he could shield her from all the sadness that existed in the galaxy.

Her mood brightened at the mention of the local populace. *'Yes, Sa. They were all nice to me.'*

Elys laughed, finishing the final bite of food. *'Yes, Scol, and nice to your belly, too. You ate two days worth of food, I think.'*

'It was all just so good. Much better than what we ate on the ship.' Learza gave him a teasing nudge through their bond.

'Insulting my cooking now, hmm?' he replied, tinging his tone with indignation.

'No, Sa, I would never do that.' The sincerity was real enough, but Elys could see through her words to the laughing warmth behind them.

'That's enough of that now,' he teased back. *'It's meditation time for you, insolent pup.'*

With a false whimper, Learza backed toward the corner, her tail between her legs.

"No, no, Learza. Dramatics will not sway my hardened heart. Off with you now, get to work." The grin across his face told Learza she had little to fear from his stoic words.

Across the room in a flash, Learza jumped on her unsuspecting mentor, catching him off guard as he lost his balance and tumbled to the floor.

"Omph! Learza!" Elys, laughing and fighting off his scolyt's wet tongue, sat up while struggling to catch his breath. "By Tir's Will, Scol, you got me good!"

Happy energy flowed off Learza in cresting waves. Nothing made her more content than seeing her mentor smile and laugh. Despite their failure to contact the Tirtet, it had truly been a lovely day.

Elys continued rubbing Learza's soft head. He would be content to stay right where they were, though he knew Tir would not allow such things until their task was complete.

"It is truly time to settle in for our meditation, scol. We've got much to do in the morning if we're to locate the Tirtet and this scion."

'Yes, Sa. I can't wait to find her!' she replied, dodging his hands and running into the common space to await the start of their meditation.

Learza's enthusiasm for their mission was undaunted by the dangers Elys feared they may face. He had to admit that her excitement was a bit infectious, though the measured balance of his Hantirri training kept him from forgetting that there were most probably dark times ahead.

Removing the cushions from the couch, the scolyt and fraer were soon settled into meditative positions, prepared to listen to the voice of the Void as it spoke of their entwined futures and the many paths they might take. A swirling energy entered their perception, pulling them from their meditation in time to hear a quiet knocking at the door.

Learza sent a ripple of worry to Elys through their bond. *'They're shielded, Sa. I can't read them.'*

'Nor can I, young one. You go behind the counter and stay there, do you understand?' Elys' tone was full of concern and Learza knew that now was the time to listen carefully to his instructions.

All their hard work on the journey was beginning to pay off. She did not argue for a second, but did as requested, hiding herself behind the counter housing the cooking area. Placing his blades within easy reach, Elys made sure they were not visible as the quiet rapping came once again from the door. Taking a cleansing breath, Elys opened the door a crack.

"Can I help you?" he asked, his tone the most controlled and polite he could muster under the tenuous circumstances.

The fruit merchant from the market stepped into the light outside the door, backed by two men who towered over her diminutive frame. She wore a tight smile on her face, but her eyes were a blank slate and Elys could read nothing from her body language. She was a closed book, as were the men behind her.

"Tir's Blesssing be upon you, fraer of the Hantirri?" she questioned. Her voice sounded as though she was most certain of who she was addressing, tinged with only the slightest doubt.

"Come in, please." Elys opened the door wider, ushering the trio inside. Regardless of whether these folk meant him harm or not, risking others overhearing their conversation made him uncomfortable.

Once they were inside, the woman took a casual glance about the room. "Where is your companion? The canine whose Blessing shines like a beacon?"

"She is none of your concern as of yet. Tell me who you are and your business with me." Elys' voice grew cold in tone at the mention of his hidden scolyt.

"You are the stranger here, it is you who must state your business, not us," the woman argued, her agitation visible in the creases at the edge of her mouth.

'Learza? I'm going to show them Gran's locket.' Elys sent the message through their bond in a subtle, quiet thread of light, hoping it would not attract attention.

Learza replied, her mental voice a whisper in their bond. *'Yes, Sa. Good idea. They might talk more if they know she sent us.'*

Reaching into his shirt pocket, Elys pulled the locket out,

careful to make his movements slow and obvious. Upon its revelation, he felt something familiar flicker between the trio of beings before him. Their shields did not quite drop, but he got the distinct impression that they meant him no harm. One of the men stepped forward and waved a hand to indicate the cushions on the floor.

"Come and sit, Wandering One, and bring your scolyt out of hiding. It seems we have much to discuss."

Chapter 14
Shadows of the past

an unknown planet, an unknown sector, somewhere in the
Shambles

The map crinkled, aged parchment flaking off its edges despite Grannie Hella's careful grasp on the ancient document. Days of travel, much of it backtracking to cover her tracks, left her tired and more than a little bit weary of her journey.

"Shoulda made a new copy o' the bloody thing. Old fool," she chided herself. "Now if I remember rightly, there used ta be a big ol' tree right abouts 'ere."

Poking the ground, she found no evidence of the great wooden sentinel of her memory. Shrugging her shoulders, Gran did the same thing she had done on numerous occasions over the last few days. Guessing she was right, she moved on, placing the map back in her pack and lifting the spade she had laid on the ground a few minutes before.

"Okay, so that's the big tree. Now I've gotta count, me, and not mess it up. Thirty paces, due east."

Her silent count began, lining up one foot in front of the other, using the spade to keep her balance on the soft ground like a tightrope walker on the high-wire. Before long the final leg of her journey was complete and she stuck the shovel into the ground where her footsteps ended.

"Well, m'dear, this is it. 'least I 'ope it is. 'Tis been many a year since I been out 'ere, and many more since ya been gone, bright one."

The warm summer air blew a gentle breeze over the elderly oracle, ruffling her traveling clothes. Placing her pack on the ground, Grannie stretched her shoulders and then began to dig, talking to the long gone spirit as she did so.

"My word, what a path yer progeny been on. No end to the wanderin' what's happened since ya set yerself and yer descendants down this crazy road. They don't go by yer name no more, dropped it in favor of another a few centuries back, though I don't quite rightly know why. T'was a good solid name, that one. Had a certain majesty to it and fit yer destiny just right if ya ask me."

Sweat began dripping down the edges of her face and running into her eyes, causing them to burn. Still, she did not slow her digging, her body pushed well beyond what she should have been capable of, given her appearance. Down, down, down she dug the hole, reaching far enough that she was forced to climb into it to continue her work.

Recent rains left the topsoil a sticky mud and it made plopping sounds as she threw it over the edge of the hole. Skrang, skrang. Glop. Skrang, skrang. Glop. The spade handle rubbed against her, the skin of her palms erupting in raw blisters, her blood melding with the wood of the handle. Face dripping with sweat, she moved forward, her boots almost pulled from her feet by the muck beneath her as she continued with her task.

Clunk. Clunk clunk. Her spade hit something hollow at the bottom of the hole. After tossing the tool up over the top, Gran reached down into the muck and traced the outline of a long, wooden box with her fingers. Removing the dirt from around its edges, she began to pry the carton loose, doing her best to avoid damaging the rotting wood as she pulled it free.

There was a loud sucking sound and the box pulled free, the force dropping Gran onto her backside in the mud with a flop. With a "Hrmph," Gran hauled herself back to her feet. Lifting the box onto the firmer ground above, she clambered out of the hole and knelt in the iron-rich, red mud.

Wiping her hands off as best she could on her soiled dress, Gran reached into her pack, retrieving a clean cloth to remove the remaining grime. Once her hands were clean, she pulled a small brass key from another pouch in her bag and inserted it into the keyhole at the front of the box.

The lock popped open freely and she reached one hand into the shallow box, using the other to push back her fraying, grey hair. A shiver ran down her spine like a cold hand on bare flesh. Gran swallowed, tears coming to her eyes as she removed the item from its container, exposing it to the light of day for the first time in centuries.

A hand, mummified and severed from its proper home, was still wrapped firmly around the cold metal hilt of a sword. Its owner long dead, this hand, shriveled and rotting as it was, represented the first in a long line of sacrifices that would bring about the resolution of the prophecy.

"Ah, bright one, 'twas yer great grandaughter whose hand this was. She was a brave one, she was, much like you. Her daughter mourned for ages, but ya'd be proud. She 'eld her own, she did. No fallin' to the temptations of the Cursed for her, no. Killed the one what did the deed in the end, but she weren't angry at him no more, just sad."

Gently releasing the limb's grip, Gran placed it back into the trunk. Clambering back down into the hole, she reburied the box and filled in the rest. Passing the blessings of the ancestors over the spade-smoothed dirt, she added a few prayers of her own for the continued safety of the dead warrior's scion.

The simple ritual complete, she then returned to the sword sitting on a clean cloth near her pack. Shining in the daylight, the hilt and scabbard appeared as new as the day they were crafted. Picking it up gingerly, Gran turned it over checking for damage, but all looked in order and it appeared untouched. She thought for a moment of unsheathing it before stopping with a sigh. She was the messenger, no more.

A grim smile passed over her face. She knew where to find the one that would wield this weapon, now she just needed to get to her in time. Securing the scabbard to her bag, she turned towards the sun. Making her way through the mud, she began the journey back to her ship, the muck sticking to her boots and sucking at her feet with every step.

Swuck, swuck, swuck, swuck...

Chapter 15
Perchance to sleep

Klen Castle, Vestra, The Shambles

Day and night were barely distinguishable at the height of winter in the north of Vestra. Though it was not yet dusk, candles were lit throughout the ancient fortress. As the never-ending winter storm swirled outside, Faza looked upon her new master with a mixture of trepidation and awe. His experience with death left him with some unnatural tendencies, including the ability to forgo sleep entirely. She could not blame him for leaving the world of dreams behind; having been at rest for many lifetimes, he was making up for lost time and she admired his stamina.

The wounds across his face could not be healed with any remedy they tried. After the third failure, he brushed off any further attempts at healing, instead embracing the marks as badges of honor. A deep scar ran from his forehead across his face to the opposite jaw line, the wound held together with visible stitches. It served as a permanent reminder that this man had crossed over the portal of the Void and came back again. It also gave an air of authority to everything he said and did in a way no other experience could have, bringing instant respect from his new subjects.

"I want the rest of my brethren raised by the next full moon. They will be most vital if they are raised before the moon's strength is at its height," he commanded, prowling across the stage where days before his body had lain awaiting resurrection. "Make the preparations. It will require willing sacrifices."

The order was given, with little regard to the reaction such a request should garner, as Naraka moved to the middle of the stage and drew a black-bladed sword.

"Yes, my Lord," Faza replied, fatigue weighing heavily upon her shoulders as she turned to begin fulfilling his request. Her own lack of sleep since his reanimation left her feeling groggy.

Departing the undead Ilandu's presence, Faza went to the spacious room she had taken as her office and shut the door, leaning against it's reassuring solidity as if it could hold her up. She closed her eyes for a moment, relishing the quiet. As she exhaled someone dove out of the dimly lit corner and grabbed her. Suddenly finding herself covered in urgent kisses, she relaxed, giving into the desperation in each kiss.

"I could have killed you, you know," she whispered in the man's ear. "You forget who you're dealing with sometimes."

"How could I forget? I'm the one who taught you how to do such things. I'm the one that molded this body into a weapon," he replied, his fervent attention never slacking off as they spoke. "I've missed you."

"And I you, Ceril," she replied, returning the attention just as urgently as he did.

A while later, their need to cling to each other satisfied,

Ceril asked her about the ritual and its success. She described it in as best detail as she could: the surprise that Naraka had been so monstrous when he first awoke and the feeling of satisfaction when his eyes cleared and he regained command of his powers and his mind.

"Asori is dead, then?" Ceril asked, no hint of remorse in his voice despite the time he had spent with the doctor.

"Yes," Faza answered, the same detached tone in her reply. "I almost felt bad for her in the moment. She never knew what was coming. Funny how a few missing pages in a journal can mean so much."

"And we no longer have to play those roles. Faza, I am glad now that things worked out, but playing the simpering sycophant is not my preferred way of working. How many nights I had to lay beside that feather-brained professor instead of at your side." Reaching up, he kissed her once more, his hands roving over her body as if he, too, was trying to make up for lost time.

"I know. I was her babysitter, her loyal friend, remember?" she replied, emphasizing the word 'loyal' with a roll of her eyes. "But that is over now and the plan was a success. Naraka is alive and well once more. The power of Tir's Will shall be ours soon enough."

"Has he made any attempt to pass his power on yet?" Ceril asked, moving to sit in a chair as he spoke.

"No, we are to raise the rest of the Ilandu before the next full moon and then he will empower us. He claims he requires the strength of his army before he will be able to perform the ritual of transference," she explained. "It is strange to see him up and moving around Ceril. He does not sleep, he does not eat. We must be careful in his presence. I can only assume that the others will be much the same."

"I see." He paced the room a moment, thinking. "I don't know if I believe his reasoning, but then I am not an expert on the lore. That is your job, my sweet."

"It makes some sense, though I do wonder about his plans as well," she replied, a thread of doubt sinking into her thoughts. "But, he is an Ilandu, the Hantirri shall fall before his blade nonetheless."

"Yes. Once the Blessed have fallen, then the Ilandu shall take control of the galaxy, just as it should have happened a century ago," he agreed, a sly smile painting across his face.

"And we shall have our rightful inheritance at last. A place of power by the side of the galaxy's greatest rulers. It is no more than we deserve." She, too, perked up at the thought of wishes fulfilled.

His brow furrowed. "Faza, dear, you must be careful how you speak of such things. This is for the glory of the Ilandu, not our own personal satisfaction."

"Yes, of course, Ceril, you are right." A knock at the door stopped their conversation. "Enter!" she called out.

"Milady, the chamber is ready." A young man informed her before giving a short bow and slipping back out the door.

Faza took Ceril's hand in hers, pulling him towards the doorway. "Come, I will take you to him."

She led him down the stone passageways as day gave way to true darkness. The flickering, dim candles throughout the fortress gave life to the stones as shadows stuttered across their surface. Pulling open a heavy, wooden door, Faza presented her lover and partner to the Ilandu seated upon a cushioned chair. He seemed to be in some kind of meditative position and for a moment she wondered if he had died again for he was not breathing.

"Roen Naraka, this is Ceril, the man I told you about," she called out and was startled when the man opened his eyes and stood up. Apparently, the breath of life would never return to him, the thought sending a shiver down her back.

"The Veasi? Ah, yes. It is good to have you at my side." Naraka gave Ceril an appraising, penetrating stare. He seemed to find something in the man that he liked, for he gave a curt nod. "You shall do well in the war to come."

"Thank you, milord," Ceril answered, giving a quick nod of his head. He took in the full horror of Naraka's presence, something at the back of his neck prickling as the Ilandu moved about the room.

"All is ready, Roen Naraka. If you would like to follow me, I will show you the rest of your army." Faza indicated a door to the side of the room and the Ilandu and the Veasi followed her through it.

Inside the cavernous room, row after row of tables were laid out. Upon each was a form under a white sheet, just as Naraka had lain only days before. Moving towards the head of the second row, Naraka lifted the fabric and took in the sight before him. A woman lay there, the pallor of death long ago given way to the green tinge of rot and decay. Some of her skin was missing.

"These people are not whole as they should be." he said,

his voice seething with banked down anger. "They will not rise whole. They shall be little more than feral beasts." He dropped the cloth in disgust.

"They were the best we could find, milord," Faza explained. "We've been scouring the galaxy for decades. My father began the search. Few besides you managed to avoid the pyres of the Hantirri."

Ceril continued, "It is hoped, milord, that you will be able to pass the Blessing of Tir on to us that we may follow you into battle as well."

Naraka turned to face them, sizing up first Faza and then Ceril. "Some of you, yes, that is possible. For now, we shall raise my brethren. They will remain under my control and will make an effective fighting force, though they will not be of much other use."

Faza hoped her next announcement would be more satisfactory to the Ilandu. "There are many who await the honor of empowering your army, milord."

Naraka nodded his head. The girl did as well as could be expected for one so out of touch with Tir's Will. "Then let us begin. This will take time and I do not wish to wait any longer."

"Yes, milord. Ceril will be assisting you tonight. I shall return to your side in the morning." Relieved that she had pleased him, she gave a short bow.

"You grow weary of my presence? Ah, yes, you are still of the living and require sleep. It has been many days now, has it not?" Naraka looked at Ceril and then back at Faza. "Go and rest then. Tomorrow I shall present to you my brothers in arms."

With another quick bow she took her leave of them, Naraka watching her back as she departed.

"She means much to you?" he asked the Veasi once she was gone, his eyes still focused on the doorway.

"As much as any woman who has been a companion for a few years," Ceril replied as he crossed his arms, making sure to keep his tone non-committal. There was no telling what information the man was searching for; his face gave no sign of emotion.

"I sense something within you that you have kept from her, am I right?" Naraka asked, continuing before Ceril could respond. "I can help you with that. I can help you discover your true potential."

Ceril hesitated. There were many things he kept from Faza, each for his own reasons. The idea of bringing this particular secret to fruition would be worth any price.

Managing to keep the excitement from his tone, Ceril replied, "Yes, milord. You are correct."

Naraka placed a hand on the man's shoulder and Ceril wondered if the gesture was sincere or simply old habit.

"Come and aid me, then, as I resurrect my brothers. You shall help me lead them when the time comes for battle."

Chapter 16
The steepness of the uphill climb

Rekitan City, Lan, The Shambles

The light scent of herbal tea wafted up to Elys's nose. He held the cup, focusing on the warmth against his hands as a way of focusing his thoughts. His visitors sat uneasily, settled on cushions before him, their deep blue robes contrasting with the drab beige of the room's walls. Sipping their own tea, the silent tension between them eased slightly as the calming herbs took effect.

The woman, called Laarni, met his eyes at last and spoke, her voice full of concern. "Only one could have sent you to find the Tirtet here. If she has not come herself, then the prophecy is in gravest danger."

Elys nodded. "Grannie Hella told me she had to attend to another errand. We are to meet up with her on Vestra after we have retrieved the Scion."

Dumbstruck for a moment, all three glanced from one to the other before Peshta, the taller of the two men, spoke. "She told you to bring the Scion with you?"

Still unable to discern the exact source of their anxiety, Elys simply nodded his head. "That was her instructions to me, yes."

They looked concerned, glancing back and forth between each other. Elys sensed a bond between them similar to the one between himself and Learza. He waited patiently while the unheard conversation continued until the man called Haerty spoke at last.

"Mistress Hella has given you a most difficult task, young Wanderer. The Scion knows not of her heritage."

Elys reacted to this bit of information with little surprise. He was beginning to understand that anything involving the secretive Tirtet was bound to mean more work for Learza and himself. "I'm sure it will be hard for her to accept at first, but surely she will have heard of the prophecy and been trained in its meaning?"

Laarni shook her head. "I'm sorry. For her own protection, she knows nothing of her destiny. In fact, she believes the Hantirri to be nothing more than a myth."

All pretense of humble acceptance of the Tirtet's limitations fell away. Elys was openly stunned by this news. The full breadth of his job now crystal clear, his brow creased in concern and frustration. He had to somehow convince a young woman that the Hantirri were not something out of legend and that somewhere out in the galaxy there was someone bent on finding and destroying her. Something told him that the Tirtet would be of little help in any of this. He sat without speaking long enough that Learza, still under strict orders to remain silent, nudged him in the shoulder to rouse him.

"You will help me explain things to her?" he asked, knowing full well what the answer would be, but hoping he was wrong.

Laarni shook her head while her companions glanced down at their teacups. "Our charge is to protect the Scion as long as she remains here. Our duties do not go beyond that and our vows prevent us from doing anything more."

"Surely you're joking." Elys' tone was no longer controlled and even. He looked from face to face and each of the Tirtet deftly avoided his glare.

With a heavy sigh, he made a final request of them, bitterly hoping that it would not be asking too much of his cloistered brethren. "Will you at least lead me to her?"

Sensing that Elys would make no further request for their help, Haerty nodded, meeting his eye. "That we can do. We are returning to our home tomorrow. She has been living with us since she was a child. You will find her there."

"What can you tell me about her?" His tea growing cold, Elys sipped it as he sat back against the cushion. The act brought him little comfort.

Learza settled her head in his lap as if she were completely calm, but her facade did not fool her mentor. Inside, his apprentice was a bundle of barely controlled questions. He stroked her head, scratching behind her soft ears as his visitors spoke, at last willing to reveal some helpful information.

"Her parents were killed in an accident when she was still an infant," Laarni explained. "She was taken under Grannie Hella's protection for a time and it was decided that she would be hidden from the galaxy."

Elys brushed the information aside with a wave of his hand as he sat up, his frustration with the Tirtet now showing plainly in his tone. "This I know. What is she like? Will she be able to handle this news?"

His aggressive approach seemed to set the Tirtet even further on edge and he thought he caught Peshta rolling his eyes. The Tirtet were known to consider their Hantirri brethren 'lost wanderers' who abused their Blessings rather than letting it work through them and Elys's headstrong reactions to their reticence was only strengthening this opinion.

Laarni's voice was icy when she continued, her tone that of a teacher giving a stern warning. "She is strong-willed and a natural-born healer. She is a good and kind young woman with dreams of having a family of her own."

Crossing his arms over his chest, Peshta finished the short description of the young woman they had raised since infancy. "She is not given to flights of fancy, she's very practical."

Another sigh escaped Elys' lips; he had not intended to set these people on edge. Realizing that his Blessing was spitting sparks of frustration towards them, he took a deep breath to center himself. When he felt that he had regained control of his emotions, he felt Learza relax as well and asked his next question.

"What is her name?"

"Tegan Asime," Laarni replied, her voice softer in reaction to Elys' revived well of calm.

Learza felt her mentor spark with recognition at the name and she watched him intently. She always found it interesting to observe his thought process, his eyes drifting skyward, his brow crinkling as he scanned his memories and smoothing subtly when he found his answer. She felt him shift uneasily; something in what he remembered sent a small shiver down his spine.

"That surname is very old, with an even more ancient heritage if I remember correctly." He wondered just how much he would have to explain to this Scion. "The Asime line came from another line, didn't it?"

Laarni nodded, impressed by the Wandering One's knowledge. Perhaps there was hope for the galaxy, yet. "Yes, she is descended from Franca Churis herself."

Chapter 17
Lady of the cloister

Road to the Tirtet Enclave, Lan, The Shambles

It was a two day walk from Rekitan to the enclave that sheltered the Scion. A grounder could have covered the distance in a few hours, but the Tirtet eschewed such advanced technology. Elys was forced to keep his sense of urgency in check, plodding along behind the cloistered monks as they made their way westward. The landscape reminded Elys of Heronat, though it was greener in this region, a few stands of tall trees scattered along their path. Learza kept herself occupied exploring, ranging almost out of sight until Elys called her back to his side. The Tirtet, with no further information to give, kept to themselves, freeing Elys to think about his forthcoming meeting with the Scion.

He had never been in a situation like this before, never trained for any scenario even remotely similar. He was one of the lowly, hard-working Hantirri, a tiny cog in the complex workings of the Diot Federation. How, by Tir's Will, had he ended up chasing threads of an ancient prophecy to the farthest corners of the galaxy?

That night as he lay on the ground attempting to sleep, his mind jumped from one idea to the next, doubt creeping ever deeper into his thoughts. He idly rubbed Learza's head as she lay curled next to him, the action had soothed him on previous sleepless nights, but tonight it was of little use.

Sensing her mentor's restlessness, Learza lifted her head, shifting over to place it on his stomach. Her deep brown eyes glowed dimly in the moonlight.

'*Sa?*' she queried, the mental nudge full of gentle concern.

'*I'm fine, Learza, go back to sleep.*' He told her, doing his best to put some authority behind his words.

'*Your mind vibrates.*' Ever persistent when she knew she was right, Learza prodded his hand with her nose.

'*You are worried, but we'll be fine, Sa.*'

Elys sighed, staring at the stars for a moment before replying. '*I'm glad you are so sure of that, Scol. I feel quite out of my depth.*'

He did not like to admit such things to his scolyt. He was supposed to be teaching her, but he knew that this journey was changing them. More and more he found their titles to be honorary. Learza was quickly becoming his equal and often he followed her lead in anything involving Tir's Will.

'*You don't see the future paths anymore, do you, Sa?*' Elys turned on his side and Learza cuddled closer, warm against his stomach. She smelled of earth and grass.

Her words sunk into his brain. It was something he knew, but had not fully understood until now. He was no longer able to walk the paths of the Void, the realization sending a shiver down his spine.

'*You're very perceptive, Scol of mine.*' Fear tinged his presence and Learza nudged his hand again until he started scratching behind her ears.

'*Don't be scared, Sa. I've never seen those ways.*' She did her best to sound reassuring, sending an extra wave of warmth through their bond. '*I was still able to find you without that help and I'm a good Hantirri, aren't I, Sa?*'

'*Yes, that you are, Scol.*' Elys could not help the smile that crossed his lips.

In the face of Learza's simple, clear logic, his doubts crumbled. Questions about the future still nagged at him, but now when he reached for the Void, he found the living energy of everything around him there waiting. Focusing on that spark of hope, the trees towering above him came into crystal clear focus, silhouetted against the star-filled sky. He could hear the worms and bugs burrowing in the ground below him and the rustling of feathers as a nightbird prepared to take flight in a distant tree.

With the sounds of the living promise of Tir's Will echoing in his ears, Elys at last fell into a deep sleep, his hand still resting on Learza's soft head.

Morning came, a bright chill in the air that faded under the warmth of the sun. With only a few words shared between them over their breakfast, Elys, Learza, and the Tirtet continued their journey towards the enclave.

The peace of sleep Elys savored for the first few hours of the day faded when the fortress-like structure of the enclave came into view on the far side of the valley. Warm red stone walls were visible under a thick layer of lush, green vines. The architecture was simple, the stone rounded and smoothed by centuries of erosion. Despite its warm, serene appearance, it loomed in Elys' vision and he felt as though it ate away at his newfound resolve with each step.

A bell in the enclave tower chimed three times. The sound was comforting, reminding Elys of the tones that rang through his own enclave, calling him to meditation. The gentle reminder that he was walking with others dedicated to Tir's Will fortified him. Calling Learza to his side as they passed between the heavy wooden doors of the gateway, Elys felt ready for whatever challenges Tir called upon him to face.

"Come, I will take you to Tegan." Laarni broke her silence, taking Elys by the arm and steering him down a side hall.

The monks they passed looked up with great interest as Laarni lead them through the enclave. Elys was highly conscious that his clothing and Learza's crystal were attracting attention, drawing the Tirtet away from their tasks. Walking a little taller, he did his best to represent the Hantirri in an honorable light.

Learza stuck close to his side as they walked through the maze of passageways. The smells reaching her nose held the fragrance of clean comfort. The few whiffs of metallic scent she detected were faint; there was little technology or industry nearby.

An arched portal in the wall lead to a neatly organized garden, flowers and herbs of all kinds grew lush and green within its well-tended beds. In the center a simple fountain bubbled, its clear water splashing the stone pathway surrounding it.

Their silent guide turned to face them, holding up a hand. "Wait here, please."

Elys watched Laarni walk some distance down the

rows to a newly turned patch of dirt. A woman was there, digging holes for a tray of seedlings next to her. At the Tirtet's approach, she looked up and smiled. As the older woman spoke, the younger's eyes ran over Elys and Learza, a quizzical look on her face.

A few moments later, Laarni rejoined them. "She will clean up and meet you in your rooms. Please follow me and I'll show you the way."

With a short, silent bow, Elys followed, Learza at his heel.

Not long after they arrived at the simple, spacious quarters that had been allotted to them, a knock came at the door. Learza bounded over to it, placing her paws up against it and issuing a short bark.

"Manners, you. You're not to jump," Elys scolded her, standing before the door.

In reply, Learza whined high in her throat and sent a wave of apology through their bond. Elys gave her head a quick rub, smiling his acceptance of her contrition. He opened the door, revealing a young woman holding a refreshment-laden tray. Shaking her hair from her face, her deep brown, penetrating eyes met his and he felt his breath catch in his throat. Feeling the blood rising to his face, he stammered for a moment, unsure what to say.

"Mistress Laarni said you have some important news for me." The woman bit her lip. "She said you've come all the way from Acking to speak with me."

Deciding she had been polite for long enough, Learza head-butted her mentor's leg, pulling his attention back to the present moment.

"Yes," Elys cleared his throat, taking a quick breath to bank down his unexpectedly rampaging emotions. "Yes I have. Will you please come in?"

Putting his hands out to take the tray, he ushered her in, Learza pushing the door closed behind him.

Chapter 18
Tearing down to rebuild

Tirtet Enclave, Lan, The Shambles

The light scent of freshly baked rolls permeated the room. Learza watched as the lovely young woman served the refreshments with simple grace, her movements smooth, and her presence serene. She wore the same basic, blue robes as the other Tirtet, yet Learza noticed she did not wear the insignia of the dedicated monks.

Elys had a strange look on his face; Learza had never seen him so nervous without provocation. Their bond fluttered, shifting and changing as he battled for control over his emotions. She could sense spikes of some new feeling which he quickly banked down, pulling his focus back toward his central core of inner calm. Learza watched as the young woman looked up, meeting Elys' eyes and she was surprised to see the light of both their Blessings flash in brilliant white, humming together on the same wavelength for a moment before Elys stood up, severing the connection.

He cleared his throat. "Tegan, please forgive me, but I need to gather my thoughts for a moment before we begin."

She nodded her head, giving him a warm smile. "Of course. I will finish here while you get a little air?"

She gestured towards the double doors that led onto a small balcony, their white linen curtains flapping in the breeze. Elys gave a short bow and walked through the doorway, indicating that Learza should stay put as he closed the doors behind him.

'*Sa?*' she reached out, brushing against his mind, and was surprised to be pushed out.

'*Later, Scol. I need a moment, please.*' Elys' tone was firm, but gentle, with an unusual note of panic.

Learza continued to worry as the light and shadows shifted erratically in the room, reflecting the Hantirri's state of mind. Noticing the concerned look on Tegan's face, she went to the woman's side, placing her head in her lap.

"Aren't you a sweet thing?" Tegan smiled, instinctively reaching out and locating Learza's favorite scratching spot behind her ears. "You're a special girl, aren't you?"

Unlike the woman at the customs booth on Heronat, Tegan's tone was not condescending nor insulting. It was sincere and warm; Learza liked her immediately.

'*Sa always says so,*' she replied. Sometimes other Blessed were able to pick up on her intent to communicate if she sent the thought strongly enough.

'*Sa? He's your teacher? Tir's Will has made you his student?*' Tegan's presence within the Blessing hummed with a mixture of surprise and delight.

Learza had been looking for more warm words, perhaps a bit more scratching behind the ears. She had not expected to start a conversation with this stranger.

'*You hear me?*' she asked, sending a pulse of curiosity towards Tegan. Perhaps the communication had been a fluke; before Grannie Hella, no one other than Elys had ever heard her true voice.

'Yes, yes I do.' Tegan nodded her head, smiling widely now. *'And there's no need to shout.'*

A few points of light glowed in Learza's inner vision. On the very rarest of occasions, Tir showed her the paths of the Void. When it did, she knew to pay it the closest attention. She could not tell where this new discovery was leading, but felt in her very soul that it was vital to their futures.

A warm glow was settling into her heart when she felt everything shift. It was as if she was plunged into a pool of cold water, the chill sucking all the joy from the room as the lights dimmed. Reaching out for her mentor, she found Elys at the center of this icy slough. She had trouble sensing him, as if he was wrapped in layers of wet wool, his presence murky.

'Sa?' she called out to him, a note of fear creeping into her tone.

'I'm fine, Learza. Do not worry.' He sent a tendril of reassurance through their bond, but it seemed weak and indistinct. *'I am a Hantirri and should not have reacted so extremely. It is better now, I have closed those thoughts down until I am free to sort them out.'*

This was not a normal reaction from her mentor and Learza found his words to be of little comfort. She had a feeling she knew what had happened to Elys to cause this new conflict and his reaction worried her. She wondered what Grannie would have done in her position.

Sensing the young dog's distress, Tegan caught Learza's attention. *'Is everything alright, dear one?'*

'Not sure.' Learza looked to the Void. Though much more muted than they had been a few moments ago, the little glowing lights were still present. *'But there is hope.'*

The quiet creaking of the doors drew both of their attentions as Elys slipped back into the room, dropping the hood of his coat back down around his shoulders. He looked more tired, more drawn, than Learza had seen him in a long time.

"My most humble apologies." He gave Tegan a small bow and sat down across from her on a low chair of woven reeds.

His tone was clear and calm, lacking any of the warmth Learza was used to hearing in it. It made her uncomfortable.

"Not a problem, though whatever just happened seems to have disturbed your student here," Tegan replied, patting the space next to her, offering Learza the spot.

Elys raised his eyebrows in surprise as Learza jumped onto the couch. He had been so wrapped up in his own thoughts he was unaware of their conversation. "You can hear Learza?"

"Yes," Tegan replied, nodding. "Yes I can. She's lovely."

At the compliment, Learza shifted closer to Tegan, placing her head back in the woman's lap. Tegan laughed, indulging the obvious request for more ear scratching. Elys opened his mouth as if to say something, then closed it once more, deciding to keep his thoughts to himself for the moment.

Tegan turned her attention from Learza and met Elys' eyes once more. "I must admit I'm most curious what you've come all this way to tell me."

"Of course. Though I must tell you this first..." Elys hesitated, adjusting in his seat. "I am about to tell you things that you will not believe at first. You may not even want to listen to what I have to say, but please hear me out."

A little shiver ran down Tegan's spine, Learza could sense her discomfiture at the Hantirri's words and snuggled closer, offering her warmth for comfort. Thankful for the gesture, Tegan continued to massage gently behind Learza's ears.

"I will listen." She nodded, sitting back into the cushion of the couch.

"You have been told of the Hantirri, the Wandering Ones?" he began, looking for her confirmation.

"Yes, they are a myth we tell the children on cold nights." Tegan nodded, curiosity evident in her tone as she ran her hands down Learza's dense coat. "I used to sneak into the library as a child and read stories of their schism with the Tirtet. They seemed to put a lot of stock in prophecy and the future welfare of the galaxy. There was one prophecy in particular that seemed most important. It spoke of a 'Daughter of the Void'."

Elys stood suddenly, pacing the floor a few times before continuing. Tegan watched him intently, wondering where this line of thought was headed. There was no reason she could find for someone to travel so far to speak of legends.

Taking a deep breath, Elys chose to speak the truth in the plainest way possible. "I am one of those Hantirri. We are not a myth."

Tegan did not move a muscle, giving no outward sign

of her reaction to his words. For a long moment silence reigned king within the room. Learza opened up her senses. Tir's Will allowed her to feel Tegan's turmoil, her desire for the safety of the enclave battling with her instinctive recognition of the truth and the adventure it might bring her.

Tegan crinkled her forehead in thought. As a child she had fantasized that one day she would meet a real Hantirri. Now that one was pacing directly before her, she was unsure if the reality was as welcome as she imagined.

A brief flicker of doubt flashed through her mind. Perhaps this man was lying and he was actually here to cause mischief. Laarni had always warned her of strangers and offworlders, but the older woman was the one who brought this man, this Hantirri, here to meet her. If he was here, he had to pass through the Tirtet elder's stern judgment. He had been lead here by the Prioress herself, giving her no reason to doubt him.

Every old story of the Hantirri she had ever read started flickering through her mind. Could they truly fly? Were they actually willing to kill others to do the will of Tir? Were they truly lost and wandering? Or did they simply find a different path to Tir's Will?

In silence, Tegan watched Elys pace. As he walked, she caught a glimpse of the hilts of two long knives secured to his back. Looking down at Learza, she watched the light glinting off the clear, blue crystal around the canine's neck. She felt along the new fledgling thread of connection she shared with Learza and a nervous smile passed over her features.

"I believe you," she said, standing to take Elys' pacing position as he returned to his seat. "And you're going to tell me that the prophecy is real as well, correct?"

With a relieved sigh, Elys gave her a single nod and watched as she continued to walk about the room. Wringing her hands, she paced back and forth, her footsteps loud and quick. None said a word for another long moment.

"And I am?" She was visibly shaking now, unsure she wanted to hear the answer to her question.

"Yes," Elys nodded. "You are the Scion in those prophecies."

"I know," she said with a sigh, acceptance beginning to replace the doubts in her mind. "Part of me has always known."

Long years of unanswered questions raced through Tegan's mind. Mysteries that plagued her for years suddenly found resolution with this simple piece of information. Laarni's face came into focus in her mind's eye. She saw the woman smiling, teaching, disciplining, always with an extra hint of worry that her pupil could not place.

"The Tirtet have been like family to me, truly." As she paced, Tegan waved her hands about. "Still, they never quite understood me. I've never truly fit in."

Elys was slightly confused by this statement. "But the Prioress assured me that you were happy here, that you desired to stay among the Tirtet until you were ready for a family."

Tegan laughed, her voice holding a hint of remorse when she spoke. "I admit I never told them the full truth. I feared I would be asked to leave and then where would I go?"

She thought for a moment, before continuing. "I had this dream, you see. There was a young man with a warm smile and a dark man with a black blade. When I was little, I told Laarni about it, but she said I should not dwell on such things, that it is not the Tirtet way to abide by visions." She sighed. "I never told her that the dream repeated itself regularly when I was awake, when I allowed my mind to wander."

Learza jumped off the couch, joining Tegan as she continued her pacing.

"I also never told them about how much I've read of the prophecy or the Hanitirri legends. Something always drew me to the library, ever searching for a missing piece of my past."

The woman smiled down at Learza, holding onto her scruff as they walked.

"There is more, I'm afraid," Elys told her tentatively.

Tegan nodded, a growing sense of rightness taking root in her belly though her hands still shook. "Somehow, I'm not surprised." She laughed, her acceptance of the truth bringing sudden joy, regardless of what the future would entail. "Come, we'll walk outside so I don't wear a hole in this floor."

Her hand still gripping Learza's fur, Tegan led them out of the enclave and across the plain as Elys told her of her destiny and all that was at stake. She was much more sober when they returned later that day, the sun setting over the top of the enclave's walls.

"We will leave whenever you are ready," Elys told her as they parted.

His voice was softer now and Learza could sense his emotional barrier thinning once more. Tegan had cried when she heard the full tale and he had reached out a comforting hand. They spoke of fear and Tir's Will and the Void, the calm center treasured by both the Tirtet and the Hantirri. His courage even in the face of his doubts gave Tegan strength and she began to feel she could face this nebulous new future.

"I will need a few days to set things in order here," she told him at the gates, her eyes still red and puffy as she smiled down at Learza. "I would enjoy spending more time with this young one, if you could be parted from her company for a bit?"

'Learza?' Elys queried.

'Yes, Sa. She needs me right now.' The answer came accompanied by a wave of love.

"Well, as I'm sure you got that reply," Elys gave Tegan a warm smile. "I will bid you two a good night."

He watched them depart down one of the long corridors towards the sleeping quarters before turning in the opposite direction. Wandering through the stone passages, Elys allowed his feet to lead him, as usual, setting no particular course for his evening ramble. A set of steps led up to a parapet and he stood leaning against the wall, looking over the valley. The stars were so bright here, unlike those few visible through the lights and haze of Torant City's technological splendor.

Watching the moon rise higher in the sky, he did his best to push back the thoughts attempting to take over his concentration. Unable to avoid them any longer, he pulled the memories of that afternoon into focus. Unhappy with the way he had conducted himself earlier, he explored his reactions, searching for the cause. Turning them over in his mind, he slowly began to accept the reason for his agitation, the flutters of joy and weakness.

With a more measured hand, he carefully banked these feelings back down under protective barriers in his mind and heart. They would do him no good in the days ahead, he reassured himself. They would be a weakness and a danger if allowed to flourish unchecked.

Satisfied that his mind was thoroughly in order, Elys made his way towards bed with a prayer that the situation was resolved and would not again rear its head.

Chapter 19
When I am king, you will be first against the wall

Klen Castle, Vestra, The Shambles

"Your army is nearly ready, milord. Should we begin planning our attack on the Hantirri?" Ceril watched his leader stroll the length of the well-appointed room, his hands held casually behind his back.

Weeks of hard work and private sessions with the resurrected Ilandu allowed Ceril some command over the powers granted by Tir's Will, but his skills could not yet help him read the mood of this man. He wondered if anyone could or if the Void had truly made Naraka something other than human. So, he waited in silence, watching the mask of calm upon Naraka's face.

"No, there is a potential threat that must be destroyed first. Any possibility that the prophecy of the Hantirri could come true must be eliminated." The Ilandu shook his head, his long mass of clumped hair snaking down his back. "Once that task is completed, we will wipe the Hantirri out of existence."

Ceril stepped forward, striding along at his leader's side as he walked. The Veasi kept a few paces between himself and the Ilandu. Naraka had either not been able or not been bothered to rid himself of the stench of his own rotted flesh. Ceril suspected it was probably the latter.

"About this prophecy, milord. Wouldn't it be better to take the Hantirri out first? Then we could pursue this Scion at our leisure."

"No. The Hantirri hold this prophecy in high regard, but they do not yet know it is in great danger. Its destruction will ensure our total victory." Naraka stopped, turning to one of the still figures that encircled the room. It shifted a little on its feet, giving the illusion of life. Unlike Lord Naraka, its glassy stare held no sign of intelligence or independent thought.

"My Ilandu brethren failed to understand the importance of this oracle, to their ultimate detriment," he said in a harsh whisper, straightening the tunic of the putrid, animated corpse before him.

"Yes, my Lord Naraka," Ceril replied with a bow of his head. "Where shall we begin our search?"

Before Naraka could reply, the sound of raised voices erupted outside the door leading to the entry hall. With a wave of his hand, the dark warrior wrapped nearby shadows around the handle and opened it. Faza entered, disheveled and red-faced. She had an old woman with her, her arms constricted by Faza's tight grip.

"I can walk quite well on me own, dearie. There be no need ta shove these old bones 'round so." Grannie Hella held her chin high, striding forward into the room, tracking mud along the fine rugs as she dragged Faza behind her.

Naraka spun on his heel, turning to his new lieutenant, his voice stern. "What is the meaning of this? Did I not tell you to keep this woman of yours under control?"

Faza's gaze met Ceril's, her brow crinkled in hurt confusion at the words, her mouth turned down in a frown. He made no move to acknowledge her and, after a moment, he turned away. When he did not speak, she bowed her head toward Naraka and began to explain the situation, her voice cracking as Ceril's betrayal began to sink in.

"Forgive me, milord, but this woman was found lurking outside the fortress. She says she's come to speak with you, though how she knew you were here, I've no idea."

Grannie stepped forward as Faza released her, an impish grin on her ancient face. "Ah, so there ye be, ya beastie."

"You dare, old woman?" Ceril lifted his head and glared at her.

"Aye, I dare, you young pup." Grannie pointed a finger at him. "And dontcha be callin' me an old woman. I'm quite young fer me kind," she huffed, crossing her arms over her chest.

"Bind her," Naraka ordered Faza, indicating a nearby chair.

"Yes, milord." Taking Grannie by the elbow, she did as commanded. When she passed him, Faza's eyes flashed over Ceril's face, searching for a sign of warmth and failing.

Grannie did not struggle, instead walking over to the chair and allowing the younger woman to bind her to it as if this was exactly where she wanted to be. Ceril quirked an eyebrow at her and she winked at him. Once she was secured, Naraka approached her, leaning on the arms of the chair so they were face to face, neither blinking.

He reached into the Void, scanning her presence and recoiling as he made contact. Momentarily losing control, his face flared in surprise and anger. The stitches holding his loosely draped skin together stretched, exposing the bone beneath.

"You come here? Why?" His voice wheezed with the effort as he concentrated on forcing air over the dead flesh of his vocal chords.

"Do I need a reason, beastie?" Grannie smiled at him, pulling back a little to avoid the odor of rot washing over her. "I go where I will, ya know tha' quite well enough, me thinks."

"My lord, why do you let her talk to you so?" Ceril stepped up next to his mentor, speaking to Naraka as if Grannie were not there.

"Have you forgotten what I've taught you already?" Naraka turned toward him, ignoring the look of revulsion that ghosted over the man's face as he admonished him. "Do you not sense what she is? Do not show me that I have wasted my time on you."

"Yes, milord." Ceril glanced at Grannie then closed his eyes. A moment later, his eyelids flew open once more, the blood draining from his face. "What is she?"

"An immortal being, formed of the very Void itself." Naraka told him, once more gaining control over the shadowed energy that kept him alive, composing his face into its familiar mask of calm. "And a rogue one at that, a force unto herself."

"Yer smarter than ye look, beastie." Grannie nodded, her head cocked slightly to the side.

She continued to smile in a way that unnerved Ceril, sending a shiver of foreboding down his back. "But then we should be rid of her, she will try to stop us."

Naraka shook his head, his calm restored. "No, she'll do no such thing."

"Tha's right, beastie. Just here to watch the show, ya know," Grannie cackled, amused at her own wit.

A roiling sense of unease settled itself in Ceril's gut. "Milord, do not let her speak."

Naraka pulled Ceril aside, his voice a low whisper as the man attempted to block out the smell of putrid flesh. "You do not understand, do you? The more she talks, the more we know."

Seeing that his words did nothing to calm his lieutenant, he continued. "She is immortal, she cannot be killed, but she only observes events, nothing more."

Grannie, still grinning madly, called over to them. She prided herself on her exceptional hearing. "Ya got that right, beastie. And when a nasty like yerself shows up, won't nuthin' stop ya but a powerful Hantirri, righ'?"

It was Naraka's turn to grin, an action that caused his stitches to spread again, turning his face into a grimacing horror mask. "You see? She gives her allies up so freely to us. Without a second thought she betrays their arrival."

He stepped toward Grannie, meeting her steady gaze once more as his voice dropped to a harsh whisper. "We will be ready for them, my dear immortal, have no fear."

"Milord?" Faza, still hovering nearby, got his attention.

"What do you want?" His voice was as dismissive to her as it was with any of the other servants.

"She carried this with her, milord." Faza unwrapped a pristine, white scabbard from a piece of cloth and handed it to Lord Naraka.

He grabbed it from her hand, his eyes flying wide open at the sight of it. Whispering under his breath, he became lost in his own thoughts. "It cannot be. No. It cannot be."

"Shakin' in yer boots, there, beastie?" Grannie cackled, thoroughly enjoying the Ilandu's distress.

Her laughter brought his attention back to the moment. He gestured at her with the scabbard as he spoke. "This blade was lost, gone forever."

As he drew the sword a few sparks shot from the edge of the blade before the whole sword turned a dull grey. Grannie winced a little as Naraka, laughing, shoved the blade back into its scabbard and tossed it aside.

"You see? Perhaps you did find the blade, Ancient One, but it does you little good. I take it you have called the Scion forth? Is she coming here to kill me with this mighty blade?"

"Aye." Grannie looked him dead in the eye. For the first time since she was brought into the room she was not smiling.

"Come, my lieutenant, we have a welcome to prepare." Breaking the deadlocked stare, Naraka stalked out of the room, Ceril close at his heels.

Neither man acknowledged Faza as she watched them leave. She moved forward, kneeling next to Grannie, locking the immortal's ankles to the legs of the chair and ensuring the ropes were secure. With the task complete, she rose and turned to go.

"Ye won't get yer wish, m'dear. It canna be done." Grannie's voice was soft, Faza almost missed the words.

Her fists clenched, she continued a few more steps before returning to Grannie's side. Her face was twisted in anger.

She stood over Grannie, spitting her words. "You lie. He has promised to share his power."

Grannie shrugged her shoulders, unintimidated by Faza's display of emotion. "No, I canna lie. Bend the truth a wee bit, surely, but it ain't in me nature to lie. T'would upset the balance ta do it."

Remembering a snippet of the recent conversation between the immortal before her and the undead Ilandu, Faza put a finger in Grannie's face. "Lord Naraka said you were rogue. You've broken the rules. What's to stop you from lying?"

"I canna go that far afield, m'dear." A quiet, understanding smile formed on Grannie's face. It was gentle and held none of the maniacal glee of the grin she used in Naraka's presence. "I jes like bein' in the thick o' things rather than watchin' from the sidelines is all. Rest o' me kind prefers to hide and jes watch. I like ta git me hands dirty. Don't change nuthin' though. Things still go as they must. Tis jes a wee bit more fun fer me is all."

Faza could not sense this being in the Void as Naraka or Ceril did, but something in her baser instincts told her the old woman was telling the truth. Her shoulders slumped slightly as she knelt in front of Grannie. She looked up, her face hopeful despite the flicker of truth taking root in her stomach.

"I suspected, but I didn't want to believe it. He can't do

it, can he? He can wake the dead, but he cannot share his connection to the Void, to Tir's Will, with me."

Nodding, Grannie put her hands out and touched Faza's head. "Tha's right, lass. Now the question is, what're ya goin' ta do with that bit o' information? Hmm?"

Without another word to Grannie, Faza stood up and left the room.

Chapter 20
All at once, not a whisper, nor word

Somewhere in the Shambles, en route to Vestra

The hilt was a strange weight in her hand, after weeks of work it should have felt more familiar, more natural, than it did. She focused on each placement of her foot, each swing of her arm. As she swung towards the makeshift practice dummy, her grip slipped and she winced at the dull thumping sound as part of a chair hit the decking. Letting the blade's tip drop, the corner of Tegan's mouth bent into a frustrated frown.

"I'm sorry. I just can't seem to get the hang of this," she sighed, sheathing the sword and dropping onto a nearby chair.

Elys also had a frown on his face and Learza looked slightly distressed.

"There is something we're missing here." He shook his head, his jaw set as he thought. "Your Blessing is more than strong enough to allow you better control than this."

"Maybe I'm not meant to be a warrior like you, Elys." She sighed again. It was not the first time they had been through this discussion. "Perhaps I'm supposed to be something else, a guide, a healer, I don't know. That's what

I was trained and prepared for, not this."

Elys sat down backwards on the remnants of the opposite chair. Running his hands over his head, he scrubbed at his scalp, leaving his hair a disheveled mess. He looked up at Tegan and she would have laughed at his appearance but for the look of determination on his face.

"I understand your reluctance, but I don't know what we're walking into. I want you to be ready in case something happens to me or Learza and we could no longer protect you."

She nodded, giving him a warm smile as Learza came to her side. "I thank you for your concern and care, Elys."

Sitting up straight, he hand-combed his hair back into place. "It is my duty. I have been charged with protecting you."

Learza was not sure if Tegan caught the shift in his tone. Where a moment ago he had been casual and engaged in their conversation, he suddenly grew more distant and removed. The adjustment was subtle, but effective. Elys' mask of Hantirri calm settled over his shoulders once more.

'Sa?' Learza prodded him, considering her own unorthodox training.

Elys hesitated before replying. *'Yes, Scol?'*

Had he been lost in his own thoughts? Learza had not sensed his distraction and the idea of her mentor hiding his feelings even deeper inside himself was bothersome. Pushing the thought aside for the moment, she continued.

'Did Tegan ever do anything else like this? Did she exercise or use any tools like that?'

Eyebrows raised as he smiled, Elys thought on her

question. *'I'm not sure, but I think you may be on to something there.'*

He relayed their conversation to Tegan. While she could hear the canine just fine, it seemed that until some sort of bond formed between the two humans of the trio, she could not hear what Learza said to Elys, nor hear his reply.

"I'm not sure," she said, standing up to walk about the hold of the ship, modified into a training room. "We used various hand tools for our gardening, but other than that, no."

"Pick up the blade again, please," Elys instructed and she did as she was told. "Now try and demonstrate some of the movements you used with these tools."

Again Tegan did as instructed. Closing her eyes, she pretended she was back in the gardens of the enclave, her rough tools in her hand as she dug out weeds and tossed them into the composting containers. When she had gone through a few of these motions, she stopped and turned toward Elys. He had a strange look upon his face.

"That was a perfect example of a Ta-Surik form," he said, shaking his head. "Please, are there any other tasks you learned from the Tirtet?"

"Yes, of course," she replied and went through another set of motions she had learned as a child.

When she finished, she looked to Elys and once again he was shaking his head, a broad smile on his face.

"They taught you all you needed to know to defend yourself."

She looked at him, confused. "I do not understand. These are farming methods, not warrior stances."

Elys nodded his head, still smiling as he jumped up and repeated a few moves back to her.

"Yes, they can be used for farming, that is true, but I recognize every step you've made as part of my own training. As acolytes, we're taught the basic history of our fighting forms. It would seem that our styles were derived directly from these old forms." His eyes lit up as he continued, excited by the new discovery. "It makes perfect sense, actually. The Hantirri were once part of the Tirtet, it's only reasonable that our methods originate with the same source."

Tegan returned his smile, she had not seen him so animated in the many weeks they had known each other. Learza, excited simply by all the excitement, barked and wagged her tail.

Elys rummaged in a nearby cabinet for a moment, extracting a section of thin rubber piping from the other spare parts.

"Here, let me see the blade a moment." Taking the hilt from her, he slid the piping over the blade, then trimmed it with one of his knives. Grasping the sword hilt, he bounced the sheathed blade experimentally on the back of the chair, and then on his own arm. Neither were damaged. He repeated the process with his knives.

"Should have thought of that before." He cleared his throat, embarrassed by his own lack of foresight.

"Now then..." He handed her back the blade and she grasped the hilt with a bit more confidence. "I want you to go through those movements again, only this time I'm going to counter-attack your moves."

She nodded, slightly uncertain this new tactic would work. Taking a stance, she closed her eyes for a moment, imagining the gardens of the enclave. Once it was clear in her mind, she opened her eyes and swung the blade. Elys blocked the blow easily, but smiled and nodded, urging her to continue.

An hour later, both were sweating with effort. The latent training passed to her by the Tirtet continued to surface as she worked. As they sparred, she began to improvise, to combine movements in an attempt to catch Elys by surprise. Once or twice she managed to almost get through his guard and he would laugh warmly and call for her to keep trying.

She admired Elys's concentration. Light gathered around him and the glow of his Blessing at the base of his throat grew stronger as they worked. Focusing for too long on what her opponent was feeling caused her to miss a step and allowed him past her own guard, one of his knives catching her directly on the shoulder.

She cringed for a second and Elys looked as if he was going to stop to check on her. His hesitation gave her the break she had been searching for and she swung her blade directly through the hole in his defense. The thin piping split and the sharp sword ripped through Elys' sleeve, cutting into his skin. With a grunt of pain, he dropped his own blade, putting pressure on the injured shoulder.

"Sorry!" she cried, dropping her sword and rushing to his side.

"It's okay. I shouldn't have dropped my guard like that. It was a good move." He smiled through the pain. "Could you bring me the med kit?"

"There's no need," she replied, biting her lip as the guilt filled her belly. "I'm a healer, remember? Now let me see it."

She helped him out of his jacket and rolled up his sleeve to examine the wound. The cut was clean and not too deep, though it was bleeding profusely. Closing her eyes, Tegan reached into the Void, following the patterns of light as she searched out the source of his pain. A moment later she opened her eyes.

"Elys," she hesitated. "There are too many garbled signals in your Blessing and I sense the tough defense you've put into place. You'll have to open up to me a bit so that I can fix this."

"You could just bring me the med kit. It's not that bad," he replied, his voice distant, his eyes focused on a point over her shoulder.

"It will not heal as cleanly or as quickly if we do it that way," she argued. "We're only a few days away from Vestra and you will need this arm fully healed when we arrive."

Elys gave a shallow nod and Tegan closed her eyes once more. The picture that filled her mind was utterly changed, she could clearly sense the bond he shared with Learza. As she pulled more light towards her, something shifted in the Void and she felt as if a thread of light wove itself between the three of them. Moving further through the Void, a wave of longing that was not her own washed over her, followed quickly by a shiver of embarrassment. She sent forth a little burst of calming reassurance before continuing on toward the pain center indicating Elys' physical injury.

Sometime later, she opened her eyes. Though the cut was still pink, new skin stretched tightly over the wound. Elys had relaxed and fallen into a deep sleep during the session, Tegan took advantage of the situation to heal a few bruises he had acquired during the course their training sessions.

His face was in the most relaxed pose she had seen it, his quiet breathing bringing a smile to her face. She ran her hand gently over his forehead and he reached up, taking it in his own and holding it against his chest with a sleepy grin.

A second later the quiet scene was broken as Elys shot up from his reclining position. He stood quickly and moved a few steps away from her as if she were something that might burn him.

"My apologies," he muttered before closing his eyes. He reached into the Void, intent on walling his defenses back up.

'Sa, no!' The shout ricocheted through the bond as Learza ran over to him and began pushing herself against him, herding him back towards Tegan.

'Scol. What is this about?' His voice was stern through the bond.

'You can't break it, Sa. You just can't. We need to be connected, all three of us!'

'What are you talking about?' He sidestepped her determined herding, crossing his arms over his chest.

'This, Elys.' A whisper of Tegan's presence entered the conversation, much to the Hantirri's surprise. *'When I was healing you a small thread appeared in the Void. By Tir's Will, it bonded you to me through Learza.'*

'Scol, did you do this?' Elys looked down at Learza, who was whimpering and pawing his leg.

'No, Sa, it just happened. It was meant to happen,' she

replied and Elys could hear the sincerity in her tone. Learza never lied to him. She truly believed this bond was destined to exist.

"Well, then there is nothing for it, I suppose," he sighed, a defeated tone in his voice. He unfolded his arms and moved across the room to take a seat.

"Don't sound so happy about it." Tegan rolled her eyes at him. "I'm sorry it's such an imposition to have a connection with me."

Her reaction caught him off guard and he stammered to correct the insult. "It... It's not like that. It just makes things more... complicated."

"In what way?" She crossed her own arms over her chest and glared at him. "I would think it would make it easier to keep in touch with each other in case we get separated or something."

"Well, yes, it would do that." He sat down, trying to understand how and when this situation had gone beyond his control. He had been so careful.

Finding the chance she had been waiting for since they left Lan, Tegan continued. "But it would make it more difficult to hide your feelings for me, correct? That's why it complicates things, right?"

"I am a Hantirri, Tegan," he told her. "We are bound to our vows. Any bond that would distract us from hearing the whispers of Tir's Will goes against that."

'But the Synod, Sa, they let us pair up. Don't we have a lasting bond?' The soft voice prodded at his mind, its weight similar to the feeling of Learza's paw on his leg.

"Learza, please." Elys' tone was sharp and biting. He

immediately regretted his outburst, but before he could apologize to his Scolyt he had to make things clear to the woman before him.

"As I explained to you weeks ago…"

She cut him off before he could continue. "Stop. Just stop. I do not need a lecture on Hantirri dogma. I lived with those that follow Tir's Will for most of my life. I know this argument all too well."

"Please, if you will let me just explain…" he argued, and watched as her face flushed red with frustration.

"Silence!" She shouted the word and made a strange movement with her hands.

Elys tried to speak, but no sound passed his lips. The sounds of the ship's engines disappeared. He could not hear Learza breathing. Even the beat of his own pounding heart did not reach his ears.

Tegan turned away and walked out of the hold towards her cabin. He chased after her, confusion written on his face. Why couldn't he hear anything? What had she done? She reached her cabin door a few steps ahead of him and closed it in his face. There was no sound, just the rush of air as the door slid on its track.

'The bond still works, Sa.' Learza's presence was shaky, a tentative pressure in his mind.

He turned to face her, bending down so their faces were level. 'I am sorry I was short with you, Learza. I let my emotions get the best of me, that was unacceptable.'

She stepped forward and nuzzled his outstretched hand. 'It's okay, Sa. I understand.'

She let him rub her ears for a moment before prodding

his thoughts. *'You should talk to her this way, Sa. I think she'll listen if you do.'*

'I can't do that, Learza. I just can't.' He shook his head. *'It would open us both up far too much. I cannot allow that bond to get any stronger.'*

Standing up, Elys walked toward the cockpit, the eerie silence still clinging to his every move.

A few hours later, the silence lifted. He wanted to go and talk to Tegan, to find out what exactly she had done to eliminate all of the sound in the ship, but he felt it was better to give her more time. Closing his eyes once more, relieved he could again hear his own quiet chanting, he returned to his meditation on the Void and the fruitless search for any clue from Tir's Will as to how he should proceed.

Learza looked up as the door to Tegan's cabin slid open. She had been napping outside, blocking the tight corridor to make sure she was not ignored.

"Want to come in, Learza?" Tegan asked and the canine jumped up, following her inside.

Tegan's eyes were red and a little puffy. Her nose was running and she blew it on a tissue as she settled into her chair. The cramped cabin held little else than the chair and a bunk, but somehow Tegan had made it feel cozy. A shelf over her bunk held a few small books of chants as well as her own journal of herbal remedies. Instead of the usual coarse blanket, a warm quilt covered the mattress and a soft blanket was draped over the industrial padded chair.

'What made the noise go away?' Learza first asked the foremost and simplest question on her mind.

"It's something I learned from an old book in the enclave library," Tegan explained. "I snuck it out of there when I was a child. It was filled with all these kinds of instructions and methods for using our Blessings in different ways. They're called Workings."

She thought for a moment before continuing. "Now that I think about it, perhaps I wasn't as sneaky as I thought. The more I access things I learned in secret, the more I think Prioress Laarni allowed me to learn them in anticipation of something like this."

Learza sat at her feet, putting her head in Tegan's lap. *'Sa was very disturbed by it. He was confused. So was I.'*

"I'm sorry for that." Kneeling down on the floor, Tegan drew Learza closer, cuddling into her fur. "I just couldn't stand to hear what he was going to say and I knew he wouldn't try to continue the conversation through this new bond."

'My Sa is a good Hantirri,' Learza replied, feeling a need to defend the man who had done so much for her. *'He has a good heart.'*

Tegan nodded into Learza's neck. "But he doubts himself sometimes, doesn't he? That's why he closes up so tight. He's afraid of failing."

Learza cuddled closer, her thoughts drifting to Grannie and her insight. *'Yes, he needs both of us to believe in him. Then he'll be strong.'*

"That's a deal, my dear friend." Tegan smiled, her nose still runny as tears welled in her eyes. "I can't help but believe in him."

Chapter 21
Feeling the weight of the world

Klen Castle, Vestra, The Shambles

How had a lifetime's worth of work made her so expendable? Faza had dedicated herself, body and soul, to resurrecting the Illandu. Training to become a warrior worthy of that legacy took decades, yet she devoted herself to the journey with no reservations. Now that Roen Naraka had risen, it seemed all her long years of dedication were meaningless.

Similar bitter thoughts floated through Faza's mind for weeks. She was shunted further and further to the background while Naraka put his grand plans into motion, his new faithful servant, Ceril, always at his side.

The lying traitor had never told her he was already Blessed, though the mark was so faint as to be unnoticeable. Every time she saw him now, she would stare at the spot just above his nose. Now that she knew what she was looking at, the mark was obvious.

She was not sure if if was fortunate or not, but she no longer saw him all that often so her opportunities to glare at him were few and far between. Ceril all but ignored her now, moving into his own quarters nearer to Naraka's main chambers and leaving her bed a cold, lonely place. Taking most of her responsibilities with him, he left her with little to do outside administrative tasks that ensured the fortress continued to run smoothly.

Since the old woman arrived, Naraka had even removed Faza from her security duties, an action more telling than any other. They no longer trusted her, though she had never given them reason to suspect her of duplicity. She may have betrayed Asori to her doom, but that had been to further their shared plans. If Naraka and Ceril suspected she may betray them as well, then Faza was in deep danger.

"Ma'am?" A man's voice pulled Faza from her thoughts.

She stared at him a moment until recognition set in. He was the latest member of the security detail. They had barely met when she had been removed from her position over him.

"Yes?" She returned her attention to the datapad in her hand.

"I can't find Roen Naraka or the Commander anywhere." His voice was tense and his breath came hard; he had been running.

"Why come to me? I don't know where they have themselves hidden. Ask the chamberlain." Eyes never leaving her datapad, she waved him off, frustration churning in her belly.

Out of the corner of her eye, she caught the man looking at his feet. "He doesn't know where they are either, Ma'am. This is kind of urgent."

She looked up at him now, taking in his flushed, disheveled appearance. His eyes darted over her face, searching for assistance. Something more important than an overflowing sink was happening.

"What's going on?" she asked.

Relieved that he had found someone with the authority to take the responsibility off of his shoulders, the man hurried to explain. "There's a ship that just entered orbit. It's not one of ours."

Anticipation flared in Faza's chest and a seed of a plan began to take root in her mond, but she schooled her face into a look of angry authority. "You should have found me sooner. Show me."

Setting off at a run, Faza and the soldier reached the communications control room in minutes. A few technicians were scattered around the room, monitoring signals from throughout the sector.

"Right here, ma'am. See?" The soldier pointed out the ship, a small craft with only a few life signs aboard. "They haven't been answering our hails, should we take them down?"

Faza shook her head, thoughts churning in her mind. "No. They're landing. Let them. Make no contact."

Another nearby technician spoke up. "You don't think they're a threat?"

With even the soldiers with no authority feeling free to question her, Faza recognized that her position was more tentative than she thought. Getting off-planet alive would take some cunning. Her voice took on a sharp edge as she replied.

"No. Roen Naraka is expecting them." She considered the plan forming in her head for a moment, then issued her orders. "Search out our missing leader and make him aware of the situation. I'll go meet these intruders myself and bring them to the main chamber."

"Yes, ma'am." The soldier gave a reluctant half bow and set off to find Naraka and Ceril.

~.~

Elys set the craft down in a clearing hidden within a copse of trees. Snow fell softly outside the cockpit, quickly covering the ship in a blanket of white he hoped would hide it from view.

Entering the hold, Elys found his two companions, their packs at their feet, preparing to go out in the weather.

"Grannie Hella did not answer our signals. I'm not sure where she is," he told them.

Tension still hung like a thick curtain between the three of them. Elys felt no need to discuss the matter of his feelings any further, reasoning that his dedication to the Hantirri was not up for debate. And so, the last leg of their journey had taken place in terse silence broken only by the most necessary communication. Much to Elys' consternation, Learza had spent most of the trip with Tegan rather than himself. He had the distinct impression that his two companions somehow considered the matter all his fault.

Tegan shrugged, attempting to hide her nervousness from him with a casual gesture. "Perhaps she hasn't arrived yet. Maybe we got here first."

"Perhaps," Elys conceded the possibility. "But something

doesn't feel right. I'm going to scout the situation out. Once I'm sure everything is safe, I'll come back for you."

"No. You're not leaving us here, Elys. We're coming with you." Tegan's voice was firm as she stood in front of the door. The edge of her long coat swirled around her feet, the wind that flowed up the ramp blew in flakes of snow that melted when they hit the warm interior of the hold.

"No, you're not," he insisted, donning his own thick, woolen coat. "You are the Scion. I'll not risk your safety."

'Sa, we're both coming with you.' Learza nudged him in the leg then walked over to Tegan, settling herself at the woman's side.

Elys pointed at his chest, throwing as much authority as he could muster behind his words. "This is still my mission, I'll not be ignored."

"I'm sure ignoring you hasn't entered their minds, but the woman is right. They will go with you."

Faza stepped up the ship's ramp, pulling back her fur-lined hood. Elys drew his knives and, in a flash, positioned himself between Tegan and their intruder.

"I'm unarmed," she said, holding her hands up before her as she stepped further inside. "Someone in my position can't afford to try something against one of the Blessed."

"And what position is that?" Tegan asked, nudging Elys aside as she stepped forward to face the intruder.

"Traitor to my own cause," Faza replied, holding her head high, a smirk on her lips. "I'm starting to make a habit of this. Doesn't mean I'm on your side, but I won't block your way either."

Elys slipped his knives back into their sheaths and crossed

his arms over his chest, hoping to give the illusion he was relaxed and in control. It disturbed him that this woman had arrived without warning. She had no Blessing that he could sense and yet, she had snuck up on them. Her mind was as still and calm as a Hantirri. The bad feeling that had settled in his gut weeks ago was getting worse.

"What do you want?" he asked.

Faza shrugged her shoulders. "Revenge always works, but for now I'll settle for passing on some information in exchange for this ship."

She put her hand up, silencing Elys' retort before it left his lips. "There are plenty of others in the fortress hanger, all in good working condition."

"Why should we believe what you're going to tell us?" Tegan asked, Learza huddled close, a tense weight against her leg. Her tail was not wagging, but she did not bark or growl, either.

"You don't have to, of course," Faza continued, glancing down at Learza. "But you'll have a much tougher time without my help."

Elys tapped the subtle bond between the three of them, utilizing their connection for the first time since Tegan's healing session and their subsequent argument.

'I say we hear what she has to say. This planet is supposed to have been abandoned. If there are people here, it would be helpful to know what we're walking into.' He put the thought forth and patiently awaited their response. He was not sure Tegan would be willing to use the connection after his reaction to their shared bond.

Learza answered first, trusting her dependable instincts

as she always did. *'She isn't Blessed, Sa, but someone here is. And I want to know where Grannie is.'*

'I do as well, Elys.' Tegan's connection was the weakest of the three. She pushed hard to make herself heard. *'I think we should keep this link open, please. I need to know what's going on.'*

After a moment's pause, Elys gave his two companions an almost imperceptible nod. Turning to Faza, he gave her a final once over, scanning her visually for any sign of a weapon.

Satisfied, he indicated a bench near the doorway as Tegan closed the hatch. "Please, have a seat."

˜.˜

"So that is where we stand?" Elys stood and paced, frowning, his hands folded before him. "Grannie Hella is captive, Roen Naraka has risen and he has an army of barely controlled, reanimated Illandu at his back. The Void has opened and spit them back out into All That Is."

Faza smirked. The woman with this Hantirri had trouble hiding her fear as the story unfolded, but the Blessed held his façade of calm. It was the one trait of his kind that she always admired.

"To make a long story short, yes."

His pacing came to a halt when Elys made his decision. "They cannot harm Grannie. I say we leave. We'll go back to the Synod and gather the more powerful Hantirri together. They'll be able to do something about this."

The uproar over his choice to run was immediate, his

companion's voices crossing over one another as they contradicted his decision.

'*Sa? We're going to just leave?*'

"Surely you're joking."

"Not at all," he replied, as if explaining something very simple and clear. "This is too big for us, it's not my place to handle something like this and my first duty is protecting you, Tegan."

Tegan frowned at him, pointing her finger towards his chest. "You were chosen for this mission, Elys. No one else."

'*Sa. She's right. That's what Grannie told us, too.*' Completely disregarding her vow to trust her mentor's judgment, Learza continued to argue the point.

"I'm not powerful enough to take on an Illandu Roen." He shook his head, hoping they would respect that his mind was made up. His companions were having none of it, their voices once again overlapping as they challenged his doubts.

"You're not alone, Elys. You've got me and you've got Learza."

'*You have to have faith in Tir's Will, Sa. We're supposed to be here.*'

"Learza, you don't know that, not for sure," he argued back, his mask of calm disintegrating as he became more agitated. Doubts about his abilities ate at him despite the words of comfort and support he was hearing.

'*Yes, I do. Grannie told me so.*' Learza clamped onto her argument like a bone, her trust in Tir's Will innocent and uncontaminated by doubt. '*And she told you, too. Tir chose us, Sa. We have to do this!*'

"We cannot do this!" Elys exploded, his voice raised in desperation. "The situation will just have to rest until we can get reinforcements."

Surprised to see the Hantirri lose his calm, Faza stepped into the middle of the disagreement. "Actually, I should correct you. You don't have very much time."

All three turned to look at her and she replied with a tight smile and a shrug of her shoulders.

"They already know we're here, don't they?" Tegan's face fell into a deeper frown and Elys slumped his shoulders.

Faza simply nodded her head. "I'm sorry to say I made my decision to defect a bit too late. They'll locate the ship quite soon. I suggest you get moving."

"And if we refuse?" Giving up their ship was the last thing Elys wanted to do. The situation was precarious enough.

Faza sighed and held up her arm, bent at the elbow and pointed at the blinking light on her wrist. "Then I'll simply call in the troops. I told them before I left that I was coming to take you prisoner. If I have to I'll go through with it and make my departure some other day."

The sense of foreboding in Elys' gut deepened as fear threatened to break through the surface of his weakening resolve. He reached into the Void, grasping for any foothold he could find to bolster his courage and still his nerves.

Closing his eyes, he could see the thread of connection he shared with Learza and, distantly, Tegan. Reaching further afield, he felt the churning anger of the resurrected Illandu Roen. His presence was roiling most unnaturally, as if it fought the Will of the Tir for every second of its existence. At last Elys truly understood why those that followed the path of the Illandu were sometimes called the Cursed. Reaching further, at the edge of this darkening storm, a globe of warm, clean light sat hovering. Grannie's voice cut through the din and darkness, reaching into Elys' heart and mind.

'Tir chose you, boy. You. Listen ta those closest to you. Love 'em, Let 'em love you. T'will be alright. Tir's Will is always...'

The voice was cut off, a wave of dark, cold energy slicing Grannie's connection like a knife. Elys' eyes flew open and he reached out, confirming that his bond with Learza and Tegan was still whole.

There was little choice left. He was a Hantirri, Blessed by Tir, vowed to help those in need and right now Grannie was in need of his protection and aid. Despite his lingering doubts about his abilities, he felt the immovable hand of Tir's Will guiding him down this path, as it had this entire journey.

"Prepare to leave," he told his companions, his calm restored.

'Sa?' Learza sent a disheartened wave of acceptance toward him.

Tegan gave him a disappointed frown.

"My apologies, I'll clarify." Realizing that they had misinterpreted his words, he smiled.

"Please prepare to go rescue Grannie and destroy the Illandu?"

Tegan looked at him, stunned, before breaking into a loud laugh. "Humor? From you? At a time like this?"

Elys shrugged his shoulders, a sheepish grin on his face.

Quickly replacing his stoic mask, he turned to Faza.

"And where will you be going?"

"Not sure. Away from here." She shrugged her shoulders, sad amusement on her face. The Hantirri were more complex and much more interesting than she had suspected, if this man was any indication.

Wrapping her coat around her, Tegan spoke, her voice softer. "There is an enclave, a place of sanctuary if you're interested."

"Work for the Blessed? No, thank you." Faza waved off the offer. "That world doesn't seem to need me, and I don't think I need it anymore. No offense, but the price is too high."

"We all need the presence of Tir, friend," Tegan told her. "You simply have to listen to it with your whole heart."

Faza frowned, nodding her acceptance of the kind sentiment. "Maybe someday, but for now I'll be fine on my own, thanks."

Faza gave a quick bow of farewell before removing her jacket and disappearing through the door toward the cockpit. With coats buttoned tightly around the two humans and a blanket tied around Learza's neck, the trio headed down the ramp and into the cold, biting winds of Vestra's icy winter.

Chapter 22
Not expecting to collide

Klen Castle, Vestra, The Shambles

The back entrance to the fortress was exactly where Faza had indicated and the codes she gave them worked perfectly. The ease of their access to the immense stone structure did little to sooth Elys' frayed nerves as the door slid open, a blast of warm air washing over him and his companions. After spending the last hour battered by the cold winds and icy snow, it was a relief to find the hidden doorway and enter into the sheltered lower level of the fortress, though he worried over what would happen once they were inside.

The corridor before them was clear and they ducked into a cramped storage closet, closing the door behind them. The space had yet to be claimed by the fortress' newest inhabitants, dust coated every flat surface reassuring the trio that they would not be disturbed. Discarding their heavy, wet coats, Elys and Tegan quickly knelt down on either side of Learza. They helped warm her feet, ensuring that all the ice was melted from between her toes, the snow wiped from her coat. She licked both their faces as they worked in silence.

Taking advantage of the quiet moment, Elys attempted to calm his racing heart. This was supposed to be a fairly simple mission, and yet it had gone so horribly wrong. He should not be the one in charge, Grannie Hella should be here to tell him what to do next. The fact that not only was she unable to advise him, but she was also a captive somewhere in the fortress simply made the situation worse. The Hantirri Fraer had no foothold here, no touchstone. He had faced brigands and thieves, assassins and haughty diplomats. None of those experiences prepared him for facing an Ilandu Roen. He hoped that they could retrieve Grannie and make their escape before the Cursed even knew they were there.

Glancing up, he caught Tegan watching him and he gave a silent sigh. There before him was the very last thing he expected on this journey. What sort of test was Tir throwing his way by placing her in his path? With each passing day, his feelings toward Tegan grew more confused. He was questioning the sacred vows he had taken when he chose become a humble Fraer of the Hantirri order, and all for a woman he had met only weeks before.

Shaking his head, Elys attempted to throw off all of his negative thoughts. With a deep breath and a whispered chant, he reached out into the Void. It was a tactile thing to those Blessed, deep and velvety and black. Like a sponge, it could be fed the fears and angers of his heart. When his mind was clear once more he opened his eyes. Tegan and Learza were watching him, both brows crinkled in worry. With a silent nod, he did his best to reassure them that he was fine and stood up, lightly stamping his feet on the floor to ward off the last of the chill.

When all could once more feel their limbs and digits, they began to make their way through the labyrinthine hallways of the fortress. Faza's instructions lead them down dank passages, dimly lit by fading and flickering yellow lamps. All was quiet as they walked up a set of stairs leading to the next level.

'Where do you think we are?' Tegan asked, thankful for the silent communication their new bond provided.

'Near the kitchens. I smell food,' came Learza's reply, her desire for something tasty filtering through their connection.

'Learza?' Elys prodded as Learza's nose flared, inhaling deeply as the noise from the kitchen's grew louder.

'Yes, Sa. I know. My tummy can wait,' she replied, apologetic as she returned to his side.

'Glad to hear it.' Elys smiled down at her, patting her back. *'Let's go.'*

Mealtime had not yet arrived, for while the kitchens were noisy with the banging of pots and yelled orders, none pushed the swinging door open as the intruders went by at a low run. Further down the hall they came to a cross-quartered hallway. Turning the left corner Elys came face to face with a small cadre of well-armed men.

"Go back, go back!" he hissed, pushing Tegan back around the corner and grabbing Learza's vest to pull her back.

"Hey! Stop!" A harsh voice called out to them while in the background another guard reported their presence into his comm.

When they did not reply, the sizzling sound of laserfire

hitting the wall reverberated through the corridor, followed by pounding footsteps.

"This way!" Tegan called out, leading them down a dark passage that looked exactly like the one they just left.

They ran blindly. Their cover blown, they no longer worried about the sound their footsteps made on the rough stone. Starting to become disoriented in the twisting passages, they turned a corner with Learza in the lead and came to a halt.

Another company of troops was waiting for them, blasters at the ready.

"Down here!" Elys pulled them both towards yet another passage, this one ending in a spiral stairway leading up.

They could hear running footsteps behind them as they mounted the stairs. Gasping for breath at the top, they found a solid, wooden door with an old, iron handle. Pushing through to the other side, Elys slammed it behind them. Tegan was already pushing on a nearby wooden cabinet and he joined her, tipping it over to block the entrance. It gave a great crash as it hit the floor, the tremendous sound of a cabinet full of breaking porcelain making Elys cringe.

"That will never hold them." Tegan gasped, holding a stitch in her side as she tried to get control over her breath.

Elys nodded, breathing hard as he tried to calm his own racing heart. "I know. It will slow them down a bit, though."

'This way, Sa.' Whining, Learza pawed at a door on the opposite wall. 'I can smell moving air.'

On the other side of the door was the main entrance hall.

All was quiet and there was not a soul in sight. They passed across its width quickly and quietly, reaching another door on the far side of the spacious hall. Elys pushed it open, ushering his companions through and considering the unguarded main door for a moment before following them.

"It's a trap." Elys told them, closing the door behind them with a solid thunk.

Tegan nodded her head in agreement. "We're being herded towards Naraka. He's in control."

Learza sat down at Tegan's feet, panting. *'What do we do, Sa?'*

"The only thing we can do, Scol. We keep going." Elys moved toward the next door, then stopped and turned to face Tegan. "I'm sorry, you should not have come here. As your protector, I should have made you leave with Faza and taken Learza with you."

'I wouldn't leave, Sa.' Learza stood, moving over to Elys' side and looking up at him.

"I've no doubt of that, Scol." Reaching his hand down, he stroked his fingers along the top of her soft head. As he spoke, his voice grew softer and more distant. He fought the fear and guilt gripping at his mind, but it was a losing battle. "But I should have ordered you to watch over the Scion and get word back to the Synod. I misjudged this situation. I've failed you both."

"You've done no such thing, Elys. We're all still alive, the last time I checked." Tegan stepped closer to him and he backed up, as if her proximity was anathema to him. It was all he could do to keep from walling his mind off entirely.

"Do you find me so repulsive? Even now?" Tegan's mouth pinched into a scowl and she poked him in the chest with her finger. "I know quite well the feelings you have locked up inside you, Elys Ki Dul. I can read your heart as well as my own."

Taking another step back, the Hantirri put his hands in front of him to ward her off. How could she see through him so clearly? When he spoke, his voice had a strangled tone. "Now is not the time, nor the place to discuss feelings. We must move on."

Tegan stepped closer and Elys found himself backed against the wall, her breath almost in his face as she fumed. "No. This is exactly the right time. We don't know what's going to happen next. We don't have control here, Naraka does."

"That is exactly why we need to keep moving." Elys argued, frustration flaring in his voice as he sidestepped Tegan and moved back to the center of the room.

"Oh, but I'm sure he'd be willing to wait a few minutes more so that I can say just one thing to you." Hands on her hips and her face flushed, Tegan painted an imposing picture. And yet, was it his imagination, or did her hands tremble slightly?

"And what is that?" Elys crossed his arms over his chest, the protective gesture doing little to make him feel any more secure.

"Simply this." She looked him dead in the eye now, and he was powerless to move. "I love you."

The Hantirri did not react. In his shock, he said nothing for a moment. His feet were no longer firmly planted under him, were they? He was sure he was adrift in some mad dream now, and prayed he would wake soon. When he spoke, his words carried little of the authority he tried to give them. "I am a Hantirri Fraer, Tegan. You know what that means."

"People change, Elys." She shrugged her shoulders, dismissing his logic. "Why can't you let yourself even try to feel anything?"

"A Hantirri releases such feelings into the Void. No anger, no fear, no worry, no regret." He chanted the litany in a wooden tone.

Tegan blew her breath out between her lips in a huff. Yes, he was sure now that her hands were shaking and he wondered what her confession had cost. "And no love, of course."

'But you love me, Sa, don't you?' Silent until that moment as the argument bounced between her two friends, Learza's tone was rife with worry.

'Learza. You are my Scol. It's different.' Elys tried to explain, his train of thought cut off suddenly.

'How?' Tegan bullied her way into the conversation taking place within the bond. Light flashed like a flare between the three of them.

'I... she...' Elys was dumbfounded, stunned by Learza's pained reaction and caught off guard by Tegan's forced connection.

'And while we're on the subject of feelings, Elys.' Undaunted by the power flowing between them, Tegan plowed on. *'If Hantirri have such control over their emotions, then why do you cling so tightly to your fears and doubts? Answer me that.'*

Before Elys could even begin formulating a response, a loud bang and a splintering crash echoed on the other side of the door they had just closed.

"They've broken through that cabinet. We've got to keep moving." Despite the danger headed their direction, Elys was relieved to escape Tegan's inquisition. He had no answer for her now, but was sure there would be a reckoning soon. The Will of Tir would make sure of that.

As if to confirm his suspicions, Tegan growled at him, her voice sharp as she opened the closest door and headed into the next passageway.

"This isn't over."

Chapter 23
Cold bravery grips my heart

Klen Castle, Vestra, The Shambles

Three more sets of guards chased the trio down three more winding passages before they were able to stop running. Tegan tried to sort her thoughts as they dashed down a corridor so wide and dark the walls were barely visible. It ended in a pair of towering, black wooden doors. Usually she was quite good with direction, but the pall of darkness enveloping the fortress, made almost palpable by the Ilandu's presence, meant she had quickly become lost.

"There's nowhere else to go but through there, is there?" Tegan said, breathing heavily.

Learza's tongue was hanging out as she panted. The dog had been quiet, for the most part, since they entered the maze-like stone structure. Tegan suspected it was fear, but worried that the dark influence of the Cursed may be somehow effecting their bond.

Elys nodded, feeling as if a tide of darkness closed in around them, pushing them toward the door. "This is it. We can't run from here."

He closed his eyes, calming his breathing, willing his heartbeat to slow to a normal rate. He could hear voices on the other side of the door, one he recognized as Grannie's, the other cold and deep. The second voice paused in its conversation and Elys felt a tendril of energy snake out and probe them. The lights in the hall grew dimmer while the three Blessed held their breath.

"You will not try to run any further, I hope." The voice was muffled, but grew louder as one of the doors swung open to reveal an old throne room.

Rich tapestries lined the stone walls and a dais sat at the far end, a simple wooden chair on top.

Elys looked to Tegan; her eyes were wide with fear, but she nodded, and as one they moved forward. Learza hovered close to her mentor's legs, he could sense her tension pulling on their bond. The trio stepped into the dimly lit room. Once through the threshold, the disturbing presence of a hundred Ilandu, brought back from the oblivion of the Void, made themselves known. Darkness washed over them, sucking their breath away as surely as it blocked the trio's vision. Shambling sideways, the Ilandu blocked the entrance as the door closed shut, an iron bolt thicker than a man's thigh sliding solidly into place.

A few moments later, the darkness faded and the lights returned, though even dimmer than they were before. Once able to recover his breath, Elys noted Grannie's position, safely out of harm's way. He also noticed that, while they were menacing and disturbing, the Ilandu that encircled the room made no move toward them and they carried no weaponry that he could see.

"So, you've gotten us here." Tegan tried to keep the fear from her voice as she took in the scarred, decaying visage of Roen Naraka. A cold shiver ran down her back as Learza moved to her side. She could feel the Scolyt quaking against her leg.

Tegan reached for their bond, trying to contact her dear friend, but received only static. Had Elys blocked her out of their connection or was this the Cursed's doing?

"You can bang on that little mental doorway all you like, Scion, but you will not be able to hide your conversation from me." Naraka smiled, the sight of his fetid visage turning her stomach.

"What makes you think I'm the Scion?" Tegan spoke more boldly than she felt. Reaching for the comfort of the light still glowing around them, she struggled to even connect with that life-giving energy in the presence of such a monstrosity. As she pulled on the gifts granted by her Blessing, a subtle glow settled around her, floating just an inch over her skin.

Naraka laughed, but it was not with mirth or joy. It was bitter, ugly laughter and Tegan took a step closer to Elys. She noticed that both he and Learza were also glowing slightly, with Learza the strongest of the three of them. She glanced around the room, taking in their surroundings, then looked up. If only it were daylight and the sun was streaming through the stained glass ceiling she could just make out, she would have taken more solace in the presence of these two trained warriors. As it was, the lights in the room flickered as if there was a bad connection in their circuits. Tegan cringed openly when one of the recessed bulbs popped and went out entirely.

"Fools. You are all fools." Naraka told them, the twisted

smile dropping from his face. "First there was that woman who brought me back from the dead, thinking I would give her the power of the Blessed. Then there was the fool who thought he would be my second in command until he could find a way to usurp my power."

Naraka swept his hand to the side, indicating the still form on the floor to the side of the dais. A pool of blood lay below Ceril's body. He turned, pointing at Grannie who sat grinning at him.

"And there is this being, carved from myth, who thinks that I cannot win this war. She thinks I have no power, that I'm an abomination. She thinks you three will defeat me, but she is wrong."

"Ya think so, beastie?" Grannie called out with a laugh, a smirking grin on her face. "Ya don't know what ye've got yerself into, laddie."

"She is wrong," the Ilandu continued, ignoring her taunts as he stepped toward the trio. "Because I can see the fear that lurks in your hearts."

He stared at Elys, daring him to contradict his statement. When Elys said nothing, dropping his eyes to the ground, Naraka laughed.

"You see? This little Scion is nothing, old one," Naraka told Grannie, his voice an echo of her taunting tone. "The prophecy will be destroyed when I kill her. Right here. Right now."

He waved his hand through the air and the Cursed Ilandu closed ranks around them. He waved his hand again and they stopped.

'Elys?' Tegan pushed at the wall around her mind. She

could feel the light flowing around them. Their bond was intact, but she could not make a connection.

She only hoped that he noticed how Naraka controlled the other Ilandu. Their glassy eyes showed no spark of life. They were mobile, rotting corpses, nothing more. She hoped with all her heart that exterminating Naraka would obliterate the rest of the Cursed as well, sending them back to the Void where they belonged. Now if only they could find the strength to destroy him.

Naraka advanced on Tegan and Elys jumped into his path, knives drawn in a flash, the blades' mirrored surfaces catching the dim light. Elys opened his connection to Tir and the Void as the subtle mark at the base of his throat began to pulse with a faint light. Pulling any bit of light and living energy he could find, he reached out to the molds and germs in the room, the trees hibernating outside, anything alive that could give him strength.

"You cannot be serious?" Naraka grinned at Elys' defensive stance. "You are a frightened, little Hantirri. I will cut you down without effort."

"You'll not get to her, not while I am still breathing," Elys told him and Tegan could hear the strain in his voice.

Light was pushing against the darkness now, the opposed forces squeezing the air around the two men like a pair of powerful magnets.

With Naraka focused on Elys, Grannie fought to get Tegan's attention, rocking back and forth in her chair and wriggling around as best she could. When the young woman glanced over, Tegan was surprised to see a sheathed sword laying next to the immortal's chair.

Snapping her foot at the hilt, Grannie sent the scabbard skidding across the floor towards Tegan. Naraka caught the movement out of the corner of his eye and turned to face her.

"Ah, the fabled Sword of Light. Once belonged to an ancestor of yours, I believe." He smirked, the action twisting his scars, revealing the bone beneath his skin. "Alas, it will not work, I have already tried to use it. There is no longer any special glow, my dear. It's bond with the Void is broken."

Tegan gazed down at the hilt, then over at Grannie, a look of confusion on her face. The Sword of Light had been lost for many years. It was said the blade could not be matched by any accept the Sword of Dark. Legend said the Sword of Light had a life and a Blessing of its own, that it was proof of Tir's Will.

Grannie said nothing in response to Tegan's questioning look, simply giving the Scion a nod and a smile. Tegan should attempt to connect with the Void through the sword. Regardless of what Naraka had just told her, the blade in her hand could connect with Tir.

The hilt felt warm to the touch, the brassy metal a soft yellow in the dim light. Tegan took a deep breath and pulled the sword from its sheath. She took a second breath and reached into the Void. Giving a little gasp, she watched in awe as the grey blade began to turn a clean, pure white, pulling light in until it glowed softly. Grannie smiled and settled further back into her seat.

Witnessing the sword's transformation, Naraka spat his words out as a curse. "Children. If you all have a wish to die, I will gladly grant it."

With a surge of crackling energy, the blade in his hand blackened until it was so dark it appeared to suck in the shadows all around it. Wielding the Sword of Dark, Roen Naraka advanced on his prey.

Unable to believe her eyes, Tegan stood frozen for a moment. She knew this blade, it haunted her nightmares when she was a girl. Made from All That Was and Shall Be, secured within the Void by the Will of Tir for the protection of all, the blade was never meant to exist in their world, the realm of All That Is. Fabled, a myth, a legend, it was impossible that she saw it here and now.

For the first time since their arrival, Tegan wished that she had listened to Elys and stayed on the ship.

Chapter 24
All systems down

Klen Castle, Vestra, The Shambles

Tegan barely had time to breathe before the blacker-than-black sword came searching for her lifeblood. Naraka's blade was intercepted by Elys, his own slick knives clashing with their foe as sparks flew.

Tegan followed his attack, swinging wildly. She didn't have time to think, to plan; her movements were chaotic unlike the schooled, controlled moves of the other two combatants. Naraka brushed aside her attacks easily, each blow nearly knocking her from her feet.

His blades darting in and out, Elys did his best to draw the Ilandu's attention away from the Scion. She could hear him breathing heavily, but she could not observe his movements, too focused on where her own feet were placed and how close Naraka's last strike had come to her ear.

'Don't worry about your technique. Just keep chopping at him.'

The voice came as a shout through their bond, catching Tegan off guard. With the Ilandu engaged in battle, he had dropped the wall that closed off their connection.

'Sa, I'm going to help.' Learza was watching from the sidelines, her presence a taught band of tension.

'*No, stay there, Scol,*' Elys ordered her, but she continued to fidget next to Grannie Hella.

'*Switch sides,*' Elys ordered.

Tegan moved to her left, doing her best not to stumble as Naraka moved forward, his blade catching the left arm of her tunic, grazing her skin. She hissed in pain, the smell of her own blood hit her nose as she ducked to avoid the next blow, gasping for breath.

Unable to contain herself when the Scion was injured, Learza dove into the fray. In the second Tegan took to regain her breath, Learza's tawny form streaked in from the sidelines. Growling and barking, Learza jumped on Naraka's back, her teeth bared savagely as she tried to get her jaws around his neck. The Ilandu stumbled forward, howling in anger and Elys' blade caught him across the chest, slicing down in a killing blow.

The strike did nothing to slow the Ilandu down. The deep gash in his chest now oozing a strange black fluid, the injury only fueled his determination to wipe them out. With a vicious snarl, Naraka reached his hand over his back, groping for Learza's collar.

She yelped in surprise as he caught her neck. A sickening horror filled Tegan's gut. She watched helplessly as Learza flew through the air, smacking hard against the stone wall and falling to the floor in front of the other Cursed still waiting on the sidelines. The contents of her vest flew in all directions, a small package tumbling toward Elys' feet. She did not stir.

"No. no. no. no. no." The litany of denial streamed uncontrolled from Elys' mouth.

Naraka took quick advantage of the Hantirri's distraction. He gathered the strength of all the darkness around himself until he was bathed in shadow, his form difficult to see clearly through the shifting fog. With a wave of his hand, the Cursed sent forth a wall of dark power, knocking Elys off his feet and sending him flying against the opposite wall, away from his scolyt. He hit the stone, dropping against the floor. Elys struggled to rise, but the blow had knocked the wind out of him, leaving him dazed. He sat back down hard, struggling to gather his mind and hurry back to Tegan's side.

Naraka let his sword drop to his side. He did not breathe and there was no sign of exertion or fatigue on his face. Except for the oozing gash upon his chest, there was no sign that he had been in a battle at all.

Tegan held the Sword of Light before her, praying the blade would somehow give her the strength and skill to defeat this invulnerable foe.

"You dare to carry your ancestor's weapon before me, Scion?" He gestured at her weapon with his own. "That blade has been defeated many times over, it holds none of the power of legend. The last owner lost her hand before she lost her life, and I was the one who took it from her. Perhaps I should start with your hand as well?"

He moved toward her, swinging his blade in a wide arc as he stepped forward. "But then she was a worthy opponent, a great warrior and a cunning adversary. You are not worthy of such a weapon. Now, I shall skip any further useless melodrama and simply kill you," he growled.

Her knees quaking, Tegan risked a quick glance at Elys.

He still sat with his head in his hands and she could not spare the energy it would take to check on him through their bond.

"Elys?!" she cried out as Naraka bore down upon her.

The Ilandu laughed. "You made a bad choice in your protector, Scion. He is weak, useless. That runt, with his weak little Blessing should never have been given the title of Hantirri."

"You lie! Elys is a great Hantirri," she yelled at him, the insult bolstering her courage.

"Then why is he on the floor and you are left alone, defending yourself against me?"

Tegan could not begin to respond. Naraka began his attack in earnest, his blade flashing so she had trouble simply following it, never mind anticipating where it would land next.

Within seconds, he had Tegan retreating towards the wall. She knew she had precious little time to muster her defense before she no longer had room to maneuver. Each time she tried to slash at Naraka, he blocked her blow with ease. He moved surefooted across the floor, dodging and weaving around her attacks before returning the volley with his own thrusting moves. She was breathing hard, her stamina pushed to its limit and her focus wavering. A flash of black passed her ear and she felt white hot pain in her shoulder as Naraka's blade nicked her, deeper this time. Thankful it was not her blade hand, the injury nonetheless served its purpose, her focus was scattered as she slashed blindly, her eyes tearing with pain.

She stepped back, her heel catching the foot of one of the

motionless Cursed behind her and she stumbled. Before she could recover, Naraka was upon her, blade blurring with speed and power. He stepped in toward her, knocking the Sword of Light out of her hands. He grabbed it, throwing the blade aside and it skittered across the floor, landing in the center of the room.

"The fate of the prophecy ends now," he told her before slashing down towards the center of her skull.

Chapter 25
Last chance to lose control

Klen Castle, Vestra, The Shambles

Bowing her head, Tegan prepared herself for Naraka's final blow. The Void opened up to her, connecting her to Tir's Will once more as her focus returned. She drew in one final breath of life, releasing it with a prayer as she felt the air move around her. The Ilandu's arms cut down toward her with horrible speed.

White light filled her eyes, the Sword of Light catching its dark twin just before it hit her head. Elys had taken up the white, glowing blade and the battle was back on, the bright blade sparking against the black as shadow and light swirled around the combatants in new, more dangerous patterns.

"You'll not defeat me, boy. I cannot be destroyed now." Naraka's taunts went unheeded.

Elys said nothing, his entire focus concentrated on the two blades and the surrounding, swirling patterns as he pushed Naraka back, away from Tegan.

Her arm throbbing and her knees weak, Tegan's mind raced, searching for a way to help the Hantirri. She could sense his determination, but under the surface she also detected his acceptance of defeat. He truly did not have the skill to defeat the Ilandu in combat and neither of them could think of a way to destroy him by another means.

The Cursed around her shifted. Unmoving until that moment, they seemed to be growing agitated by something. Tegan looked around but saw nothing unusual until her eyes fell upon Grannie Hella. The old woman was watching the battle, but sensing Tegan's gaze she glanced over to her, giving a subtle wink.

Confused, Tegan watched as Elys backed into retreat once more, closer to Learza's motionless form. A pang of worry slammed through Tegan's heart as she watched the blades clash. His stamina was beginning to fade, he would not last much longer. When he was a few feet from his beloved scolyt, Grannie called out to him.

"The package, boy! Throw it at the ground!"

Naraka turned as if to say something to Grannie and in that the split second, Elys reached down and grabbed the small bundle Grannie had slipped into Learza's vest all those weeks ago on Acking.

Naraka laughed, returning his focus to Elys and the object in his grip. "What is it, my immortal? A little bomb, perhaps? Think a bit of explosives will destroy me?"

Elys hesitated, looking toward Grannie for confirmation. Was he was about to blow them all to pieces? She simply repeated her command, her voice calm and polite.

"Throw it at tha ground, Elys. Do it now, please."

"Yes, Hantirri," the Ilandu taunted, lowering his blade. "Do that and we shall see who rises when the dust clears."

Elys closed his eyes as he slammed the object to the stone

floor. There was a bright flash of light and for a second he thought he truly had blown them all up. When his vision returned he found himself, along with Roen Naraka, at the center of an iridescent dome of light. Through the translucent barrier he could see Grannie smiling and Tegan uncovering her eyes.

Naraka said nothing. He did not move, the Sword of Dark dropping from his hand, clattering and dispersing its shadowy power as it hit the ground. The spark of unearthly light that lived behind the Ilandu's eyes was gone and he crumpled onto his knees.

Elys reached out for his connection to the Void, but found an empty chasm instead of the comforting warmth of its embrace. Tir's Will did not sing in his mind. The dome closed down his Blessing and blocked out both connections. It was as if the only thing that existed was All That Is, there was no balance of power, no future nor past, only the present moment. The energy of momentum, of life and movement was gone, including the energy keeping the Ilandu's soul locked into his decaying body.

The sword in Elys' hand glowed brighter now, returned to the forge that formed it. This blade was of a time, not a place. With a few swipes of the sword, Elys carved up the rotting remains of Roen Naraka, dismembering his limbs and removing his scarred head. When the gruesome task was complete, he moved to the edge of the dome. It gave way easily to his blade's stroke and he ran forward, only one thought now on his mind.

He dropped the blade to the side, carelessly discarding it as he fell to his knees at Learza's side.

"Learza?" he called to her, lifting her head. When Tegan reached his side, she heard his voice crack as he called his friend's name.

He reached out into the Void, his control lost with his grief, he plunged blindly, searching for any sign of her warm, cheerful presence. *'Learza?'*

She stirred slightly, his urgent calling drawing her out of her unconscious state.

"Let me see her," Tegan soothed, tears threatening to break free from her eyes. She put one of her own shaking hands over his. "Elys, please, let me see her."

Relenting his hold on his dear friend, he allowed Tegan to smooth Learza's fur, examining her head.

"She's got quite a bump, there's a lot of swelling. Let me just…" And Tegan's words faded as she shifted her focus inward.

Elys sat back on his heels, unwilling to leave Learza's side. He listened to Tegan's soft chanting, the words and the energy they brought soothing his own frayed nerves so he, too, could focus inward and find his calm center.

'Sa?' the gentle nudge warmed his heart. *'I'm okay, Sa.'*

With a great sigh, Elys released a breath he hadn't known he'd been holding. *'Scol. I thought I had lost you.'*

'Not me, Sa.' Elys opened his eyes as a soft tongue brushed over his bruised knuckles.

"Naraka is gone. Now what do we do?" Tegan met his eyes, the fatigue of her fear and confusion sinking into her bones as she slumped next to him.

"I guess we…" He was cut off by an urgent shove from Learza.

'*Sa!*' He felt her shaking with fear and looked at her to find her eyes rotating wildly.

"What is it?" Tegan asked.

Learza jumped to her feet, Elys and Tegan scrambling to follow her. '*The Ilandu, Sa!*'

They turned in a circle, looking all around them. The undead Ilandu, now free of their master's strict control, were converging on the trio. Decomposing arms reached for them, a low, groaning sound leached from ragged lips as cold, dead eyes watched their every move.

"Grannie!" Tegan called out, panic in her voice. Somehow they had to get past the Ilandu to free her.

"It's you they want, child, not me. Run!" she yelled to them.

Elys blasted a wave of light toward the nearest Ilandu, punching a hole in their ranks. He tried to grab for the Sword of Light as they ran for the door, but the Ilandu were moving quicker now, sensing their prey's attempt to escape. Their rage intensified as the trio avoided their grasp, the Cursed jostled and shoved each other, chasing the trio out of the chamber.

"Go! Go! Go!" Elys yelled, pulling Tegan and Learza out of the nearest doorway and into an unfamiliar corridor.

Chapter 26
Beauty in the breakdown

Klen Castle, Vestra, The Shambles

Every bone in her body was aching, she was fatigued, and her emotions were raw, still Tegan kept running. She could see Elys' jaw clenching as his mind worked, seeking some way to get them out of this situation. Their first priority was a safe escape and after that, a way to destroy the horrible creatures now hunting them.

The Ilandu sped along the corridors, never more than a few seconds behind them. Tegan struggled to keep the vision of their deteriorating bodies out of her mind's eye, fearing that their ghoulish, rotting features and empty eye sockets would haunt her nightmares for years to come. She took a brief second to wonder how Tir's Will could allow such abominations to exist in the realm of All That Is before returning her full attention to their flight.

Since leaving the main audience chamber where their leader was destroyed, the Cursed were eerily silent as they followed the trio. Even their footsteps made no sound. Learza risked a glance back as she ran, pacing her two companions.

'What's making them follow us, Sa?'

"I don't know." Elys was at the back of the group, keeping Tegan and Learza in front of him.

The high, arched corridor had no doorways along its length, the smooth stone coming to an end in a T-shape that opened into two opposing hallways.

Learza arrived first, sniffing in each direction, but unsure where to run next. *'Which way, Sa?'*

"Doesn't matter." He pushed Tegan forward. The Ilandu had just turned into the end of the corridor. "We just need to put some space between us and them so we can come up with a plan."

A door stood open at one end of the intersecting corridor and Learza ran towards it, Elys and Tegan close on her heels.

Once they were all inside, Elys slammed the door shut, dropping the wooden crossbar into place. He turned around to see panic flashing in the eyes of his companions as they scanned the room. It was a storage space, but one that had fallen into disuse. Completely empty, the room had no other exit. Putting his ear to the door, Elys listened for any sign of the Ilandu, but heard nothing on the other side.

"I don't know if they followed us or not." Elys reached into the Void, trying to isolate the corrupted presence of the risen Ilandu, but the unnatural nature of their resurrection left no ripples in the dark waters of his mind.

Tegan wrapped her arms around herself as she tried to calm her breathing. "Let's assume they're following me for some reason, drawn somehow to my position as Scion. If that's true, then I'm sure they're out there."

Sorting through all the swirling emotions in the room,

Learza cut through their fear and clarified their situation with her simple logic. *'How do we destroy them, Sa?'*

"Good question, Learza." Walking the perimeter of the room, Elys searched for loose chinks in the masonry. Perhaps with some concentrated effort, they could break through one of the walls with the gathered light of the room. "We've got no weapons, not that it seems to matter. If Naraka was any indication, blades alone are not going to get the job done."

Tegan stood still, her eyes unfocused, thinking. "It's got something to do with a Working. That's how they were brought back from the dead."

"Yes, when that dome of energy went over Naraka and I, our connection to the Void was cut." Elys paused in his inspection, picking at a loose stone until it came free in his hand. "Tegan, is that something you can do? You were able to throw that cloak of silence over us on the ship."

Tegan did not answer right away, considering the question. A spike of hope jolted through their loose connection, fading just as quickly as it appeared.

"That's just sound manipulation. It's much simpler." She shook her head. "Whatever allowed them to be brought back from the dead is much more powerful than that."

'You know a way.' Learza prodded, bumping her head on Tegan's leg. She sensed the woman's reluctance to share her thoughts.

"Perhaps," she admitted, a note of dejection in her voice as her shoulders slumped. "But the consequences are enormous and it wouldn't work anyway."

Walking back to his companions, Elys urged her on,

seizing the glimmer of hope. "The consequences mean little at this point. They will kill us if we do not at least try to destroy them. What is this way? How does it work?"

Looking down at Learza for a second, and then raising her head to face him, Tegan gave Elys a long stare as she considered her words. With a quick, determined nod, he encouraged her to speak. Closing her eyes with a sigh, she pulled out a small metal blade, it's sharp edge glinting in the dim light. She stared at the floor when she spoke.

"We would have to spill a bit of blood from all three of us. Not much, just a few drops." She looked at her companions again and when neither said a word, she dropped her eyes back to the floor and continued. "Then we draw the light in, all around us, forming a tight circle. When the Ilandu enter, we send the gathered light at them, like a bomb, emptying ourselves of it entirely in one big, concentrated wave."

Elys considered her words for a moment, sensing there was some component of the Working she was leaving out. As he was about to question her, a loud thumping sounded against the door. All three looked at it, then each other, a spike of fear filtering through their bond.

Elys swallowed hard, returning his attention to his question. "It sounds dangerous, but not impossible. Why won't it work?"

Pulling her stare away from the door, Tegan sighed, shaking her head. "The only thing that will keep us alive through that kind of Working is a strong bond, Elys. Ours is not powerful enough to withstand it. It's scattered, frayed and you've denied it any growth. We'd all die."

Optimism flowed from Learza. Despite her fear, she held strong to this new hope. *'We can sure it up, can't we, Sa? Our bond is strong, wouldn't that be enough?'*

"No, little one, it wouldn't be." Tegan shook her head again, reaching down to sooth Learza's raised fur.

Silence fell between them when a sharp bang echoed from the door. Lost in her own sense of dread, Tegan was caught off guard when Elys spoke.

"We can make it work." Elys said, his voice soft, unsure. Something shifted in the Void and he sensed possibility and life at the end of this journey, despite the claxon of death pounding on the door.

Looking at him with confusion in her eyes, weeks of frustration boiled over and Tegan snapped back at him. "What are you talking about? We have nothing here, Elys, nothing! You've made quite sure of that, holding yourself so distant from me. Blocking me out of every conversation you have with Learza. Keeping all of your feelings trapped behind that Hantirri wall of reserve."

Elys stepped closer to her, something coming to life within him, sending his heart rate up until his blood thundered in his ears. He put out a hand toward her face and she could see it trembling.

"Elys?" He claimed a Hantirri did not know fear, but she felt his terror as it filled him.

His hand moved, ever so gently, brushing away a tear she hadn't realized she was shedding. They froze and Tegan was unsure what could possibly happen next.

"It is time," Elys spoke, choking the words out with a voice sounding nothing like his own.

He moved closer to her, his breath warm against her face and she could hear him struggling to maintain his control as he shook from head to toe.

Closing his eyes, Elys reached into the Void, looking for reassurance, for answers, but there were none to be found. He was at a precipice, a crossroads. His entire life built up to this single moment and he knew this decision would change the course of the future for more than just himself and Tegan. There was no answer to his plea for guidance, the voice of Tir's Will remained a silent presence as he made his decision. There was no longer room for his nagging doubts, no more space for excuses, the responsibility for what happened next lay firmly on his shoulders. With that realization, the air seemed to clear and his breathing slowed. If the decision was truly his own to make, then the choice was simple and clear.

Cupping Tegan's face ever so gently in his calloused hands, he tilted her head up as he bent his own down and their lips met.

She was soft and warm, pressing closer to him as each second passed. The light and shadows swirled, twisting around them and their bond opened wide, the threads of connection clinging to one another, braiding into a tight, unbreakable rope of energy. When they parted her eyes were glistening with tears and he was smiling.

"So we have a bond then," she laughed, putting a finger over his mouth as he began to speak. "Ah, there is much to discuss, I know. You are a Hantirri, after all. But let's get out of here first and we'll figure out the rest later, shall we?"

His silent smile broadened and taking her hand in his,

he nodded his head in agreement.

Learza growled at the door, her hackles up. Her presence in their bond was swirling with nervous anticipation. *'They're coming through, Sa.'*

"Everyone here." Tegan walked to the center of the room, jumping into action.

Drawing the knife lightly across the back of her arm, she winced in pain as red blood welled to the surface. Elys put his own arm out and she repeated the action. He gave no reaction, the chorus of Tir's Will once more singing in his ears, its song full of joy, despite their desperate situation.

Learza whined a little as the back of her own paw was cut. In the center of the floor between them, they allowed their wounds to bleed, a small puddle of blood forming in a depression in the stone.

Focused now on their work, they barely heard the splintering sound of the door beginning to buckle. Kneeling together around the blood, they held onto each other, Tegan chanting a repeating litany of words foreign to the others' ears. The words mattered little now, as they were caught up in the whirlpool of energy they pulled from the dim light around them, every cell in their bodies stretched to the limit of endurance as the room grew darker, the ball of light before them increasing in intensity.

The door shattered with an ear-splitting crack and gave way. Ilandu began pouring in, heedless of their fellows as they made their way toward the well of light energy, desperate to suck from its life-giving juices.

The trio's power built to a thunderous head, their minds screamed for release as the power overtook them. Releasing the ball of light, it blasted from them, a wall of white-hot flame and energy shot out in every direction, shaking the foundations of the fortress as it exploded over the Ilandu.

The Cursed collapsed under the onslaught, their rotting flesh burning to dust as the wall overtook them, turning their bones to ash as they fell.

The power faded as it burned out, leaving a vacuum in its wake. Their effort leaving them little more than empty conduits of the light, the trio collapsed to the floor, the Working taking the last of their energy as it obliterated the final Ilandu.

Chapter 27
And in the end

Klen Castle, Vestra, The Shambles

A soft hand rested on Elys' forehead. It was cool and soothing, a gentle energy filtered through his body, rousing him from unconsciousness. His eyelids fluttered and he stirred. Every part of his body had a dull ache, his very bones felt as if they had been leeched of life.

"Jes you lay there a bit, laddie. Take yer time gettin' up now." Grannie's voice was soft and soothing as her hands.

Despite her warning, Elys was anxious to check on the others. He raised himself up, leaning on his elbows as the room began to spin.

"Tha's alright then, don't listen ta yer betters when they talk sense," she scolded him, clucking her tongue against her teeth.

"Tegan, Learza, how are they?" He put his head to his hands, determined to rise and tend to his family.

He stopped abruptly as the thought crossed his mind. Family. That is what they had somehow formed without his noticing. Realization of what he had done began to sink in. He could not remain a Hanitirri, he had chosen to leave that path when he kissed Tegan and forged their bond anew. There was no turning back.

The idea did not fill him with the fear and doubt he would have expected of such a decision. Instead, he felt lighter, buoyant, and his heart was full. All his years of searching for that hidden, elusive thing that would calm his discontent faded to the background. He tried to use his Blessing, anxious to connect with the gentle power of Tir's Will and see that it gave affirmation to his choice, but he found he could not use it any longer.

His brow crumpled in concentration and focus, but no matter how hard he tried, he could not feel that greater presence in his mind.

"It's gone," he whispered.

"The Blessing? Aye, laddie, ye canna use it no more it seems. Tha Working burnt it out of ya mostly. Kept ya all alive though, din'it?" Grannie's gentle hands helped him into a sitting position.

"Then they're okay?" he asked, his mind returning to his first thought. Family.

"Why dontcha take another look a' that ol' Blessing, see if there ain't somethin' left there?"

Elys reached in once more, searching for any feeling of connectedness to the larger universe around him. The silvery rope of energy that connected him to Learza and Tegan came into view. He followed its path, winding through the utter blackness that surrounded it until he could feel his family's presences, warm and waiting for him.

'Learza? Tegan?' he was tentative, unsure if they would be able to hear him.

'We're here, Sa. We can hear you.' Learza's warmth shone

through the bond, she was happy and her tail was most probably thumping against the floor.

'We don't have much else, Elys, but it seems Tir has left us with this.' Tegan's presence was soft and warm.

'I don't think I need anything else.' Elys admitted as he rose, his head clearing at last.

"This way, young one." Grannie lead him through the corridors, back to the main chamber where the many pieces of Naraka's body were still laying on the floor.

Tegan hobbled toward him as soon as he entered the room, Learza walking beside her. It seemed his two dearest companions had not fared much better than he had. He wrapped Tegan in his arms and they stood leaning against each other for quite some time. After spending so much effort denying his feelings for her, he now found it difficult to let her go.

"Well, my children. The task is done and I thank ye fer all yer help." Grannie gave them a little bow. "Les clean up this mess and get on our way."

In the courtyard outside, they lit a pyre and burned the remains of Roen Naraka, ensuring that he would never rise again. The rest of his people seemed to have scattered for they encountered no one along the way to the hangar.

There were a few ships available, just as Faza had told them. Naraka had been stockpiling them so that even though his people fled in all directions, there were still a few to choose from.

The journey back to Acking was peaceful, though filled with discussions and planning. It was decided that for the safety of the prophecy, the Synod would not be notified of the nature of Elys and Learza's 'sabbatical' and the twinned swords of Light and Dark would travel with them back to Lan and the hidden Tirtet enclave.

A few comm calls once they were within the Diot enabled them to schedule a meeting with the Synod upon their arrival. Unable to wait any longer than they had to, as soon as they arrived they made straight for the Priory. As they were about to mount the stairs to the main entrance, Grannie stopped them.

"This is as far as I go, m'dears. I've no desire ta enter tha' building."

Tegan stepped forward, wrapping Grannie in a warm hug. "Thank you so much, for everything."

"Ah, tis no trouble at all, dearie. Yer worth yer weight." Grannie smiled. "And na jus because yer the Scion. Yer a good girl."

'And me, too?' Learza stepped forward, nuzzling Grannie's leg.

"Yes, wee one, ya most certainly are a good girl." Grannie laughed, bright and clear in the cold air as she scruffled Learza's head. "You be keepin' an eye on that Sa o' yers, ya hear?"

Learza barked her response and stepped back as Elys stepped forward to face Grannie.

"Ah, laddie. I do apologize fer what ya had ta go through here." She felt a bit remorseful for all the pain and trials he had to endure, even if it was for the best.

Elys shook his head, a quiet smile on his face. "No, Grannie. Please do not apologize. I have found my true path, one I never could have imagined."

"And ye seem ta have found a bit o' confidence in yerself ta boot." She smiled at him.

"I certainly hope so," he replied, his voice deadly serious. "I have to face the Hanitirri Synod and tell them that I've fallen in love and I'm leaving." His serious mask broke as a broad grin replaced it.

Grannie was surprised when he stepped forward and wrapped her in a big hug. "Thank you," he whispered, then released her.

Clearing her throat, Grannie smiled broadly, blinking back something that must have gotten in her eye. "Well, I've got pittins that'll be wonderin' what happened ta their supper if I don't git meself off." She gave them each a once over and a nod as she turned away. "Don't ya be worrin' though. I'll have me eye on ye."

They waved and watched her until they could no longer distinguish her white hair in the shifting crowd.

"Are you ready?" Tegan turned, looking at both Elys and Learza in turn.

"I don't think I can ever be ready, but now is as good a time as any," he replied, sighing deeply. "Let's get this over with. Then we can go home."

Offering his arm to her, he lead the three of them up the staircase and into the main entrance hall of Steeltip Priory. As they walked through the cavernous space, he pointed out statues to Tegan, explaining what he knew of the history of the Priory. Crossing the floor, they became aware of the stares of the other Hanitirri around them. Their clothes were bedraggled, torn and dirty, yet they walked, arm in arm, heads held high. Tegan whispered something in Elys' ear and he laughed, his mirth echoing off the stoic columns of the main entrance.

Elys' mood became more subdued as they rode the lifts to the Synod chambers. Tegan kept her arm linked in his, her head rested lightly on his shoulder, oblivious of the stares of the other Hanitirri sharing the lift with them.

Arriving at the chambers, Elys made sure she was comfortable on a bench outside the doors. She kissed him on the cheek and he smirked, straightening his scruffy clothing as he turned toward another of the Hanitirri who stood staring at him.

He smiled as she approached, bowing to her. "Sa. Thank you for coming."

"What is going on, Elys? I barely sense your Blessing. What has happened?" Hepsi Tan's face told of her worry for her erstwhile Scol.

"I have found my true path, Sa," he replied, pleased to find that the bond he shared with her still remained as well. "Learza and I will be leaving the Order."

"So you have brought me here to say goodbye?" she asked, her tone full of disbelief.

He nodded. "Yes, and also to give you these." He detached the scabbards of his long knives from his back and tried to pass them to her, but she pushed them away.

"Your blades?" she asked, her tone growing even more concerned.

"Yes, Sa. I would like you to pass them on to the next scolyt who seems out of their depth," he replied, smiling at the memory of the day she first gave him the sleek blades.

"Elys?" she asked, confused as she met his gaze and

found him staring back, his eyes full of a confident fire she had never seen before.

"Truly, this is what I wish, and what I am meant to do," he whispered, taking her hand and placing the blades in her grip.

When she looked as if she would question him further, he stopped her with a raised hand. "It is the Will of Tir, Sa. Do not look for any further answers than that, for I do not have them to give."

Accepting the truth of his words, Fraer Tan gave him a deep bow. "Goodbye then, my Scol." She gave him a bemused smile as she turned away. "The Blessing of Tir's Will be upon you."

"And on you, Sa," he replied, watching her back as she left.

Feeling Learza leaning against his leg, he looked down at her. "Well, my dear pup, this is the last time I shall be calling you 'Scol'."

'I know, Sa, and I've been thinking.' She nuzzled his hand. 'You can just call me Learza if you want to, but I can't call you anything but 'Sa'.'

"And I think you shall always be my Scol in some way." He smiled down at her. "We'll keep this one thing then."

'Okay!' Learza barked aloud, her joy like a cresting wave through their bond. 'Ready, Sa?'

"As ready as I'll ever be, Scol," he replied and, with a final tug to straighten his shirt, he lead Learza into the Synod chambers, the doors sliding quietly closed behind them.

Second Edition Bonus Content

As part of this second edition, I've included some bits and pieces that are part of the foundation for the story you just read.

I hope you enjoy this deeper glimpse into Elys and Learza's world.

Sins & Salvations

A series of snippets that give a peek into how Elys and Learza first met. They are based on Ben Franklin's 13 virtues, which I used as a basis for the tenets of the Hantirri Order.

"TEMPERANCE. Eat not to dullness; drink not to elevation."

Elys watched with concern as the puppy ate. She devoured the food, oblivious to anything else around her. It had to be her first meal in days. After a while, her belly started to bulge a bit and he pulled her away from the bowl. She whined and cried as he wiped stray bits of food from all over her head.

"That's quite enough, pup. You'll get sick if you each too much in one sitting."

He was rendered speechless when he felt a pressure on his mind and a single word, like a whining pout, in his head.

"Hungry."

"SILENCE. Speak not but what may benefit others or yourself; avoid trifling conversation."

His first mission was a disaster; there was no way around it. Not only had Elys failed to make his drop off on schedule but his return trip was dragged out three different times by bad weather. If he had simply checked the reports, he could have avoided any delays. It was during his second delay that he stumbled upon the puppy now tucked in his bag, asleep.

"Anything to declare?" the irritated voice of the customs agent roused his attention.

"No…" Elys gathered himself quickly, his lie needed to be convincing. "Nothing."

The official nodded and stamped his papers.

"ORDER. Let all your things have their places; let each part of your business have its time."

Meditation was an important, in fact integral, part of Elys' life. It was the way he kept control of the powers gifted to him so that he would not become a danger to others around him. This was the lesson he had been taught since he was a small child.

The only problem was that this disciplined existence did not factor in a small, rambunctious puppy with a determined mind of her own. Rather than meditate, Elys found himself cleaning up after his new companion and doing his best to keep her quiet and entertained on the long journey home.

"RESOLUTION. Resolve to perform what you ought; perform without fail what you resolve."

"So it seems you are not quite ready to handle the tasks we expect of you."

Elys stared at his feet. He knew he should have his head up, meeting the eyes of the Synod circled around him. Embarrassment kept his gaze on his boots.

"Yes, sir." He mumbled in response.

"You will spend two weeks here, reviewing the Books of the Blessed & Cursed. We will decide your next mission at the end of that period."

"Yes, sir." He turned to leave, but was called back by a woman's voice.

"Keep your chin up, boy. You can handle this."

"FRUGALITY. Make no expense but to do good to others or yourself; i.e., waste nothing."

"Leos Tan, does something trouble you?"

Hepsi Tan smiled at the acolyte. Bright and energetic, the girl was the opposite of her previous student.

"I have noted Leos ki Dul behaving strangely of late and it worries me, that is all. He takes extra food when he thinks no one notices and twice I have seen him wandering the halls when he should be meditating."

"They have whispered in the acolytes' quarters that he is not his usual reserved self."

Leos Tan frowned. If the acolytes were paying attention to the young man's actions, then something was definitely going on.

"INDUSTRY. Lose no time; be always employ'd in something useful; cut off all unnecessary actions."

What am I doing? This is foolish. Why did I take such risks bringing this puppy to the priory? We will get caught and then what shall I tell the synod? What will Leos Tan think of me?

I should give her to someone who can care for her. What business does a fraer have with a pet? They are frivolous attachments.

All day I think these things, praying I do not get caught before I can decide a course of action. All night she cuddles at my side and I know I must find a way to keep her.

"SINCERITY. Use no hurtful deceit; think innocently and justly, and, if you speak, speak accordingly."

"You will think me foolish, Leos." Elys sat on the stiff-backed chair, his hands tucked into his sleeves. His voice did not falter and Hepsi Tan wondered if her former charge rehearsed this speech, for his words were more succinct than any he had uttered before.

"I promise I will not, Elys. I have known you far too long to think you a fool."

"There is something special about this dog, Sa."

Hepsi sat back, considering the puppy next to her former student. She was unusually quiet for one so young, and seemingly glued to Elys' side.

"Tell me more."

"JUSTICE. Wrong none by doing injuries, or omitting the benefits that are your duty."

We discussed the various implications of young Leos ki Dul's claims. He was not known to draw attention to himself and we took his past record into account when presented with the evidence of his deception.

He would not be allowed to keep the dog as a pet, of course, but she did seem to have some unusual qualities. When the test results came back we had no choice but to do what was right for them both. They would not be allowed to leave the priory for some time, but they would become teacher and student just the same.

"MODERATION. Avoid extremes; forbear resenting injuries so much as you think they deserve."

Aching, pounding pain clouded the young man's vision. With a heavy sigh, Elys at last admitted to himself that they would have to stop for the day. In contrast, Learza was enthusiastic and ready to continue, her wagging tail thumping against his thigh.

He knew she was trying to talk to him, tell him something, but the bond between them was still too tenuous for him to filter her thoughts into words. He was not blessed with gifts strong enough to bully his way through this, they would have to pace themselves and pray that understanding would come in time.

"CLEANLINESS. Tolerate no uncleanliness in body, cloaths, or habitation."

"I realize that she is a dog and this might be natural for her, but I do expect you to keep some kind of control over her."

The matronly woman was a full head shorter than Elys, yet she managed to present herself as the tallest person in the room.

Nodding, he mumbled a string of apologies as he knelt and began sweeping up the dirt and broken bits of clay. Learza cowered behind him, tail between her legs. He turned to her after the woman left.

"I know you understand me so please listen when I tell you no."

"TRANQUILLITY. Be not disturbed at trifles, or at accidents common or unavoidable."

Pacing the floor of their room, Elys clenched his fists in frustration. Two weeks of solid effort, some of the hardest work he had ever done, and all he and Learza could communicate to each other was the slightest hint of their emotional state.

"We're going for a walk." He announced and headed out the door, Learza at his heels.

The dark quiet of the priory at night soon soothed his frayed nerves, quieting his mind.

"We'll find a way, Sa." The voice in his head held a steady calm. "We have to."

A broad smile spread over Elys' face.

"CHASTITY. Rarely use venery but for health or offspring, never to dullness, weakness, or the injury of your own or another's peace or reputation."

For the first time since they were cloistered months ago, Elys and Learza were sent on a mission. Granted, it was simply going to the market to purchase spices for the kitchens, but Elys treated it as a solemn responsibility.

They had to pass through one of the red light districts to get to the market, an unfortunate result of rapid, ill-planned growth. Ladies and a few young men teased the duo as they made their way down the street.

Elys blushed, taking what solace he could in his vows and the string of cold links around his neck.

"HUMILITY. Imitate Jesus and Socrates."

"Sa, why do we sit back here?"

Over time Elys was becoming accustomed to the soft pressure on his mind. Learza's 'voice' in his head could best be described as emotion and thought somehow instantaneously translated into words. With experience it became simple to discern Learza's communication from his own 'inner voice'.

"We do not wish to draw attention to ourselves." He explained to his charge as everyone settled into their seats. "The front is a place of honor for those who have earned their position."

"But what about the middle rows?"

"We are not worthy of that place yet."

Her Mother's Voice

*A short story featuring Grannie Hella and
one of Tegan's ancestors. This is Grannie's first
appearance in my writing.*

*A modified version of this story was published in
the anthology "The Shining Cities" published by
Bibliotheca Alexandrina.*

Walking with head held high, the young, dark-haired woman strode down the dimly lit street. Her heart was pounding as she trekked down darkening passages, the crowds thinning the further she walked. Towering buildings blocked the sun from view as soon as she descended into the middle levels.

The lower levels of the city were notorious for being the most dangerous territory around, still, here she was, strolling down the narrow lanes, squinting her eyes in search of her elusive quarry. When she reached the middle levels a few hours ago, it was just past noon. Here in the depths, only an hour later, even the bright afternoon sun barely trickled down, leaving these levels in perpetual twilight.

Finally recognizing the district she was looking for, her pace quickened. Hope was slim that the person she searched for would even be alive, never mind still living in the same place, but a small, tight smile appeared on her face when she saw the old woman putting out plates of food for the alley felines that circled her feet.

"Greetings, Grannie Hella." She called out to the elderly figure. "I've come to speak with you and… I need to speak to someone else as well."

The grey-haired woman did not acknowledge the younger one, but went about her task as if no one was around. Having been well instructed on how to approach Grannie, the young woman waited, squatting down to pet the striped feline that was rubbing her ankle.

"Name, girl?" came a short, croaky question.

"Tamora Umbeki, madam." She replied in her most polite, proper tone.

"Hrmph. Vela's child. I know what you want then. You chose the proper evening, too. Good thinking, girl." She gave a very heavy sigh and stood to look Tamora in the eye. She was taller than Tamora expected and her back showed no signs of bowing with age.

Grannie rattled on in her thick voice, "Work's never done for your clan, is it? You'll be needing to know there'll be others wantin' to speak with you, too. Not just yer Mum. Come on then, and don't let any of these critters in the door, they'll wreck the whole thing."

Tamora nodded her understanding and followed the woman inside a rusty door, carefully closing it behind her so none of the felines snuck in. The tight corridors of the ancient building gave off the stale scent of mildew and decay. Following Grannie closely, she soon found herself in a dingy, but orderly dining area with a dark wooden table in the center, dominating the room.

The old woman brushed her hands on her apron to clean them, then moved about the space, clapping three times in each corner before returning to the doorway. "Well, we'll be needin' a right, proper meal for this. What you got in that basket?"

Tamora placed the large basket she'd been carrying on the table and opened the lid so Grannie could see inside. Various containers were stacked neatly inside and the light aroma of gourmet cooking wafted out of the cramped hamper.

"Yes, good. That'll do nicely. Ever been through one of these before?" Grannie questioned. Tamora shook her head and the old woman cackled. "No? Your Mum taught you proper, though." She reached up and pinched Tamora's cheek with a gentle squeeze. "Let's get started then. Night will be falling soon. And remember, no talkin' til you get the sign or I tell ya so."

The two women set to work in silence as they spread a black cloth across the table. Grannie pulled out heavy, black place settings from the cupboard as Tamora removed the sturdy black anodized utensils from a box on the sideboard. The table completely set, the food was unpacked and heated through in the small kitchen. After placing the bowls and platters on the table, Grannie and Tamora sat across from each other, leaving the head of the table empty and shrouded in dark fabric.

At a signal from Grannie, Tamora served the dessert onto the three dishes. Though her nerves turned it to sawdust in her mouth, Tamora politely ate her entire serving. She watched Grannie closely, but the old woman simply ate her food with a comfortable smile, obviously enjoying the decadent layer cake. The main course came next; meat so tender it melted on the tongue accompanied by herb-dressed vegetables and soft, boiled tubers. Again, Tamora watched for any signs from Grannie, but the woman was obviously relaxed and enjoying the rare treat.

As Tamora was about to ladle some brothy soup into Grannie's bowl, the old woman's arm shot out and grabbed her hand, pointing to the end of the table. Stunned, Tamora looked at the place setting and watched as a thread of mist rose from the plate and coalesced into a glowing, blue ball of light hovering over the chair. Next, a similar thread from the meat joined its brethren and Grannie quickly motioned for Tamora to serve the soup.

By the time the bowls were filled, the hazy, yet visible features of Vela Umbeki solidified into form. She looked down at her hands, then glanced around the room and smiled.

"Tamora, I did well in my instructions if we are seated here today." The warmth of her smile brought long-dried tears to Tamora's eyes. "Yes, my dear, you may speak now, but do not allow your soup to grow cold." the woman indicated with a gesture that Tamora should continue eating.

Unable to help herself, Tamora let the soup spoon fall from her grasp. "Mother, I've missed you so! All these long years, I've wanted to talk to you, but knew I had to wait. I..." the words were almost a sob, but Tamora took a breath. She knew their time was limited and there was much to say. "I have news." She hesitated and her mother gave her a knowing smile.

"It's a child, isn't it?" Tamora spoke softly to her crying daughter.

"Yes." She returned the smile. "I shall name her Noma, after Nomidan, your mother."

The smile brightened on Vela's pale lips. "It is a good name and she well do well by it." the translucent figure continued, regret in her tone. "I am sorry I cannot be there to give the proper Lifetelling, my child. All I can Tell you is this, she will forge her own path. Her ways are not to be our clan's ways. When she is grown, a man will come who walks the Fire path. He will give her great joy and great pain, but he is the key to her destiny. You must not bar that path."

Torn between joy and grief, tears streamed down Tamora's face. "And am I to maintain the traditional silence, even through she leaves the clan?"

"Yes, daughter. She will not understand why you let her go so easily, for she shall be young, but the Lifetelling is only for the mother to know. It is the burden of our clan." Her voice grew weaker with each word as her figure lost its strength and clarity.

"Mother!" Tamora cried out as Vela's figure faded quickly from its place in the chair.

"I can always hear you, child, just speak and I will know." Came the final echo of a whisper as the last of the strange blue light faded to nothing in the candlelit room.

Tamora slumped back into her chair, placing a protective hand over the slight bulge on her abdomen as she did so. Silence once again took hold in the room for quite some time, though it now lacked the heady excitement that charged it before.

Once Tamora's tears dried, Grannie finally spoke, softly and with a clearer tone than younger woman remembered her possessing. "It is done, then. The course has been set. The Waterstrider shall fade and the Firedrifter shall inherit and all shall give way to Earthwalker."

Tamora stared at the woman and made a sign of blessing toward her.

"Oh, don't waste you're time with that, child. I'm not

possessed by some Daemon. These old bones know things, is all. 'Tis my fate, young one. I've watched it all come and I'll watch it all fall. Some would say it don't make life worth livin', knowing how it ends, but I just can't wait to see how it all plays out. I'll be there when she completes her tasks, I'll watch those children grow and I'll be there when they return to the Void."

Grannie reached across the table and took Tamora's hand, gently patting it to calm the young woman, garnering a weak smile in return. "Now, if you've had enough of a break, let's finish this lovely meal and see who else turns up, eh?"

Tamora gave her a hesitant smile as both women dipped into the warm, soothing soup and watched in wonder as the seat at the head of the table glimmered bright blue in the darkness once more.

The World of the Hantirri

*A bit of information about the world
where the story takes place.*

*Just some definitions of the special titles
and words found throughout the book as
well as a little bit more about the special
abilities of those with the Blessing and
Curse of Tir's Will.*

Terms

Fraer: fully vested member of the Hantirri or Tirtet order

Ilandu: the heretics of the Hantirri who broke off and waged war against the Diot

Mika: a high official of the Hantirri

Roen: a high official of the Ilandu

Sa: affectionate term for teacher, used by a student

Scolyt: term of address for a student of the Hantirri or Tirtet order

Scol: affectionate term for student, used by a teacher

Synod: a priory council of the Hantirri, the Grand Synod is the high council

Veasi: warrior clans of the Shambles

Vostra: representative of the Zemvo

Zemvo: the Diot Federation's ruling body

Locations

Diot Republic – where most of our story takes place, a collective of 22 planets

Torant City – the capital of the Diot Republic

Acking – the capital planet of the Diot Republic

Lan – Planet on the edge of the Diot, where the Tirtet have secreted the Scion

Vestra – headquarters of the revived Ilandu cult in the Shambles

Kinet – secret home of the hidden Sword of Light, located somewhere in the Shambles

Heronat – home of the Tirtet enclave that hides the Kapradina diary, in the Morlan sector

Stone Sanctuary - main temple of the Tirtet on Heronat

Pendar – a planet in the Yarran sector, the location of Elys and Learza's first mission

Steeltip Enclave – headquarters of the Hantirri

Klen Castle – headquarters of the revived Ilandu on Vestra

There are 22 planets/moons in the Diot Republic. There are also 15 settled planets/moons in the Shambles. Many once belonged to the Diot, but were abandoned during the course of the wars and plagues.

The Nature of the Blessing and Curse of Tir

Blessings are gifted at random throughout the galaxy. Many of the non-Blessed are members of other religions based off the belief in the existence of Tir and the Void.

The Blessing (and Curse) leaves a mark either on the forehead (psychic abilities) or the chest (emotional, healing abilities), sometimes both. The darkness of the mark indicates the level of power. Elys's mark is not that dark and in both places, Learza has a darker mark on her chest.

Powers of the Blessed tend to be psychic in nature, the Cursed utilize the more physical elements of their abilities.

The Tirtet is the hidden branch of the Hantirri. They separated during a great schism 2,000 years before, at the start of the Ilandu wars and moved to a planet that was abandoned by the Diot's Zemvo.

Powers granted to the Tirtet and Hantirri:
- precognition, with control over following the path
- object reading, touching something and reading past events or about the person that held it
- healing, both of physical and emotional/mental/spiritual wounds and illnesses, without tools

- limited telepathy

Powers granted to the Ilandu:
- bone manipulation
- accelerated healing
- fast reflexes
- enhanced basic 5 senses

Powers available to all Blessed or Cursed:
- ability to sense other blessed/cursed
- manipulation of darkness (Cursed) or light (Blessed) as physical objects

Diot history

The Ilandu Wars lasted for 1,500 years and were followed by a great plague. The Ilandu were comprised of a heretical sect of the Hantirri who used the power of the Blessing in order to try to take over the Diot. Up until this time, no one outside of the Hantirri knew what those Blessed were capable of doing.

The standing army of the Diot was quickly overwhelmed by the Ilandu, and the Zemvo begged the Hantirri to help them. The Hantirri did as requested and began to train themselves for combat. It took time, a generation grew up and passed on before the Hantirri were able to redirect their peaceful, healing energies into the power needed to defeat their corrupted brothers.

The Diot Republic began to shrink as people moved back towards Acking and the less-scattered protection offered by the Zemvo armies.

A final standoff occurred between the two Tir sects and the Ilandu were defeated. By this time, the Hantirri had taken control of most of the government (as it was offered to them to ease the process of war) and they had a difficult time returning to their cloistered ways.

Their peace was short-lived as a few years after the war

ended, a great plague swept through the Diot. Once again, the Hantirri were called into action, this time in their traditional role as healers.

We visit the Diot a century after the end of the plagues. The Hantirri have been kept on by the Zemvo as healers, messengers and bodyguards of the ruling body.

Offically, they are called heroes, the saviors of the Diot. The public, and even some members of the Zemvo under their protection, fear the power the Hantirri are capable of wielding.

Despite all weapons, except for their basic swords and bladed weapons, being taken from them, the Hantirri are not openly trusted.

Other notes

Naraka carries the Sword of Dark. Grannie retrieves the Sword of Light, its companion and the sword that felled Naraka the last time he was killed.

The Hanturri gave up all but their bladed weapons when they gave control back over to the Zemvo. The weapons were used to reinforce the standing army of the Diot.

The oldest Hantirri are about 150 and were alive when Naraka last walked the land. They awake or cry out in nightmares when Naraka rises, but no one pays it any mind.

The translation of the chante Asori performs during the ritual:

Tir is all and Tir is one
Tir come raise your fallen son
Death and life reverse the twain
Make this warrior whole again

About the author

A pixel-slinger and code monkey by trade, Jennifer Lyn Parsons is a life-long lover of story with a capital S. Her work has been seen in *365 Tomorrows*, *Dark Valentine Magazine*, *Eternal Haunted Summer*, and *The Shining Cities Anthology*, among others. She published her first novel in 2012. When not writing either code or fiction, she runs Luna Station Press, devours comic books, and sometimes makes things out of wool. She can be reached through her website, jenniferlynparsons.com.